THE DEVIL TAKES

ALSO BY FAE

SPOOKY BOYS SERIES

Bite Me! (You Know I Like It)
Possess Me! (I Want You To)

STANDALONES

Let Our Hearts be Light

FREEBIES

There's a Monster in the Woods
Cloudy with a Chance of Dildos

THE DEVIL TAKES

FAE QUIN

Cover Art and Interior Artwork by Fae Loves Art

WWW.FAELOVESART.COM

Typography and Interior Formatting by We Got You Covered Book Design

WWW.WEGOTYOUCOVEREDBOOKDESIGN.COM

Editing by Angela O'Connell at Indie Author Creative

WWW.INDIEAUTHORCREATIVE.COM

DEDICATED TO MY HUSBAND

for being the reason I believe in soulmates.

For anyone who needs a book to escape into.

Haden

Percy

Useful Terms While Reading

Scent blockers: Medication used to block scents—both internally and externally—causing what is commonly referred to as scent-blindness.

Suppressants: Medication used to stall oncoming heats. Intended to be used in small batches and not for an extended period of time.

Slick: Natural lubrication omegas produce when aroused.

Knot: A protrusion around the base of an alpha's dick that when aroused can tie the alpha to whoever he has mounted for a period of ten to twenty minutes.

Presentation: When an alpha/omega hits puberty and their hormones send them into either Rut, for alphas, or Heat, for omegas

Heat: A full heat is a two-to-four day period of time where an omega is producing more pheromones and slick than normal while the body attempts to attract a mate. Sometimes can lead to pregnancy. Heat lengths vary depending on the person and occasion. Omegas can be thrown into a false heat when they meet their fated mate.

Fated Mates: A term used to refer to people who are physically and emotionally more compatible than anyone else. Can often be used as a symbol of status. I.e. a couple who claims to be fated mates has more status than a couple who does not.

Alpha-hole: A commonly used insult referring to alphas.

Knothead: A commonly used insult referring to alphas.

Blanked up: A slur used to describe an omega who is on scent blockers, and therefore smells like a beta.

Mating Gland: A gland located on the trapezius that is bitten during mating. When biting occurs, souls are linked and if the bond takes, the couple becomes bonded.

Bonded: When two souls connect positively after a mating bite has been initiated.

A full list of content warnings and tropes is available on my website:

WWW.FAELOVESART.COM

ONE

PERCY

It was cold.

The kind of cold that takes bites from your flesh and burrows deep inside the marrow of your bones. Icy. Mean. Painful in its winter flavored vitriol.

If I'd been a smarter guy, I would've been at home, tucked safely inside my dorm room on the wrong side of campus. I'd be staring at my always studying roommate—like I did every night—wondering why the hell I'd gone to college in the first place when I knew I'd never fit in.

Instead, I was naked.

Dirt clung to my knees and shins, and my toes and fingers were numb.

The scent of dead things permeated the air so strongly that even I could smell it. Rotting leaves and decay, like an exhale between winter's first harsh, life-sucking kisses.

The sun had sunk below the horizon ages ago.

But stubbornly, I didn't leave.

1

I listened to the whistle of the wind, shivering, as my cock shriveled up and the hair on my thighs did nothing to warm the tremble of my quaking limbs.

I was stupid.

I'd always known I was stupid.

Hell, I'd been told it enough times that in my mind it had become just another fact. But even knowing that—for me, *this* was a new low.

Tales of myths and monsters had kept me awake for days in preparation for this moment. So, I couldn't help myself as I stared at the gaping hollows between tree trunks, searching through the darkness for the passage beneath the bridge I knew lay hidden in the shadows. At any other time of the year, it was just an ordinary underpass.

Not today.

Not for long.

At least if the rumors were to be believed.

They said the Devil came out on autumn nights just like this one. That the passage to Hell was only a few short steps away, hidden behind tombstones and half-wilted bouquets at the back of a graveyard older than the town itself. They said the Devil visited those that were most vulnerable. They said the Devil took what he wanted to take.

Just like any rumor I'd heard whispered between my peers in crowded classrooms, I'd disregarded this one.

When the brothers' fraternity had suggested this as initiation, I'd laughed along with all the other guys. It seemed a small price to pay if it meant winning a permanent spot in the frat house starting the next semester.

They said the Devil only took what you were willing to give.

I wasn't willing to give much, so even though one by one the other

freshmen had fled when the sun had bled blue, I stayed behind.

Stay the whole night.

Naked.

Fail to stay, and you forfeit.

Those were the rules.

Maybe it was stupid to risk my life for this, but, hell, I *was* stupid. The kind of stupid that no one notices till they ask you a question and get to watch your blank-faced confusion as you scramble to understand what they'd even asked in the first place.

Unfortunately for me stupidity wasn't my only weakness.

I wasn't particularly great to look at either.

I had no skills to write home about, unless you counted artfully avoiding my roommate's attempts at painting my toes.

Thick-bodied and untrained, I was athletic, sure, but not in the way that turned people's heads, or cushioned my dad's empty pockets. Too big to look the way I was "supposed to." Too small to look the way my dad wished I did. About as dangerous as a rather large bunny rabbit.

All of that, plus I was hiding the fact I was an omega from ninety percent of the population?

Yeah.

The only thing I really had going for me was my desperation. *I needed this.* Needed that room more than I was willing to admit, all my faults be damned. Without the money to pay for it this was my last and only option.

So, stubbornly, I stayed. Even though my nipples were hard and my pecs trembled with each painful, icy breath.

Was this even safe?

Was hypothermia a thing you could get just from wind alone?

Recognizing that those thoughts would only lead to madness, I swiftly put a stop to them. Maybe being stubborn would save me from the cold.

Maybe not.

Either way, I stayed.

Each breath hurt more than the last. My lungs expanded, then shriveled up tight. The cold choked its way down my throat as I stared into the darkness and waited, and waited, and waited.

God, the sun was taking forever. What an asshole.

Maybe I could go home early?

Maybe they wouldn't know?

Maybe I was just making excuses.

Maybe by staying I was just as stupid as everyone always said I was.

Maybe I'd die out here, only the wind for company, the frost eating my frozen stiff flesh.

Macabre.

A French word I only knew because I'd Googled it on one of the library computers after my roommate had used it in a sentence I didn't understand. Though, what I'd Googled was *Mah-cob*. So, I was surprised I'd gotten a result in the first place.

To distract myself I watched as the moon climbed high in the sky, its pale silvery light creeping through the bare limbs of the bonelike trees that bracketed the gateway to Hell. Funny that people called it that, when I knew the truth. Hell was waking up every day knowing there was nothing you could do to end the nightmare. Hell was craving the love and attention of the people that would never stop hurting you. Life was Hell.

4

Despite what Tommy said, I was a realist, not a pessimist. (Another word I had to Google recently.)

"Hello?" I called, because sitting in silence was almost more painful than the cold.

Predictably, there was no answer.

My cheeks tinged red with humiliation. I swallowed my tongue.

The wind whistled.

An owl hooted.

The stars glimmered, then dodged behind a passing cloud.

"*Hello.*" The simple reply was spoken so quietly I wasn't sure I hadn't imagined it. It crept around me, made of creaking tree limbs and mausoleums. Drafty as the bitter breeze. Low. With good humor. Curiosity too.

Hello.

Had I imagined it?

Maybe.

Maybe the cold was driving me crazy.

Maybe I'd used the word maybe way too much tonight.

I wasn't sure I would be able to move, let alone run, should the voice be anything but my imagination. It wouldn't be that surprising if I wasn't alone tonight. If there was something far scarier hidden deep within the woods than a devil that didn't show his face. In a town as small as Madison, you'd think the likelihood of something dangerous lurking inside the woods would be low, but I wasn't sure I believed that. There were probably serial killers in the woods. Hunters of human flesh. Alphas ready to take things that weren't theirs. To bite what wasn't theirs to bite.

"Hello?" I called again, the deep timber of my voice glancing off tree

trunks. I waited.

Each breath forced its way through my trembling lungs. My pulse thrummed.

"Hello." Again. The voice wrapped around me, louder this time, sweeter. A quiet purr that sounded too close to flirting to make me anything but terrified.

Stupid omega.

Something I'd been called more times than I could count.

Stupid omega.

Stupid omega.

Stupid omega.

"Are you lost, omega?" The voice was clearer this time, an accent lilting through words that tasted like tart berries bursting on my tongue. The base of my skull tingled, the mating gland on my neck throbbed. That voice was…it was—

It was.

"I'm not lost." The words choked their way out of my throat, catching on the breeze as I moved—stiffer than I would have liked—trying to spot who was talking to me. I didn't see anyone, though. Only graves. Only leaves. Only the gaping hollow beneath the barren cobblestone bridge.

"You are cold," the voice observed.

I still couldn't see anyone.

Fear made my pulse sluggish, my knees weak.

That voice though—

It rumbled up inside me, causing an avalanche of emotion. My thighs trembled as my cock gave a feeble twitch despite the cold. Heat, unlike anything I'd felt before, began simmering under the surface of my skin.

Bubbling, bubbling, bubbling.

I had become so used to the dull numbness of the suppressants and scent-blockers I took, that the influx of new sensation nearly blinded me.

"Creatures as pretty as you should not be bare." The voice caressed the shell of my ear, tickling its way inside me till my insides burst with light and the cold shriveled away, almost like magic.

I'd never been called *pretty* before.

Burly, sure.

Hot.

Dumb.

Useless.

But pretty? No.

I glanced around again, still searching for the owner of the voice, but instead, all I found was a low throaty chuckle that made my toes curl and my lashes flutter. Slick. I was *slick*. I could feel the way it dripped down my thighs, my ass cheeks rubbing, my breath coming in panicked little bursts.

Was the fear breaking through my suppressants?

I'd never had fear as an arousal trigger before.

I still didn't. Probably, anyway.

I wasn't sure what this was.

And then I saw him.

It.

That.

The shadowy depths of the desolate bridge gave birth to a tall silhouette. Lean. Dressed in inky black shadow that sloughed off like water as he took step after step out of the darkness and into the silvery moonlight. The more he was illuminated, the clearer his figure became. Not because

7

he was getting closer, but because the moon leeched the magic from him like bleach on blood.

From a distance, all I could see were bones. They decorated his shadowy silhouette in an illusion that made him look like he was nothing but a skeleton whenever he stepped into a puddle void of light.

He wore a mask in the shape of a human skull that lit up silver as his long legs led him out of the tree line. And as he stepped closer and a beam of moonlight hit his face, I realized if I squinted, I could see his eyes behind the hollows of the mask. The first thing I noticed should've been obvious. Even from a distance I could see that they weren't human. Inverted colors. White where they should be dark, black where they should be light, his irises glowing softly.

Devilish, just as the stories had warned.

My cock throbbed and a whimper burst unbidden from my throat. The cold had now been chased away entirely by heat. My body thrummed with nervous energy, sweat beading across my temple as my knees trembled and I glanced down, for just a moment, only to spot the already dripping tip of my throbbing dick.

Fuck.

Precum leaked down my crown, slicking the pink surface, and I reached down without thinking, ready to squeeze till I eased the pulsing ache of desire. I stopped myself just in time, grabbing my thigh instead, my nails biting into the frozen-stiff muscle. I had company. I didn't really want skeleton dude to see me jack off, no matter how badly I wanted to.

Consent was a thing.

It was bad enough I was already naked and needy.

Only a second had passed, but when I glanced up, the skeleton dude had crossed a surprising amount of the distance between us. He now strode across the rocks that edged the graveyard, though his steps were silent.

He was taller than I'd first guessed. And the closer he got to me, the more he began to make sense. He wore a uniform—not unlike a military uniform—though his was covered in silvery-white embroidery that took the shape of the bones I'd spotted even from a distance. Detailing on the fabric caught the light as his long, lean figure strode confidently across the grass. The skull shaped mask he wore cast shadows over his eyes as dry, dead leaves crunched beneath his tapered leather boots. I could hear his footsteps now.

Crunch, crunch, crunch.

Was this a trick?

It felt like a trick.

A Halloween prank gone wrong?

Or had the Devil come to take what he was owed?

I'd thought I didn't have much to give, but as my cock jumped and my hole gave a needy twitch, I realized I'd been wrong. There was a buzzing in my ears, a fog in my head, a heat coursing through my body that I had only ever felt once before. A whine built up in the back of my throat unbidden. A primal sort of sound, a call for something I didn't have the words to put a name to.

"Hush." Ten steps away became nine, then eight. Long legs moved leisurely, muscular thighs flexing as the Devil came closer and closer. Distantly, I wondered if this was my fault. If I'd invited him here by calling a greeting into the darkness.

For a second, nothing felt real. The world was full of possibilities. My waking nightmare was forgotten as he stopped only a few feet away. He

was so close I could count the silver beads etched across his uniform. But instead, I did something I'd never done before. I checked him out. Staring at his thighs made my dick twitch, my hole clenching as my gaze dragged upward. Though slim, there was no doubt that he was all man. His shoulders were broad, his jaw, where it poked out beneath the mask, square. With compact hips and thighs that should not be as supple as they were—I was lost.

I didn't need to smell him to know that he was an alpha.

That didn't stop me from trying. I inhaled greedily but his scent was as masked as mine. Though I doubted his was chemically stunted. It was more likely it had been swallowed by the same magic that had coated him with shadow. Which wasn't to say that finding no trace of him in the air, even with my nose twitching and my toes curling, didn't make my heart ache.

The lack of scent was *jarring*.

Wrong.

A needy feeling I didn't recognize trembled like butterfly wings in my belly.

I wanted to plead, but he'd told me to hush.

The quiet command, husky with no room for disagreement, had done things to my already squirmy insides.

"What do you want?" he asked, dipping at the waist. He was so close I could've stared into his eyes. I could've admired his broad shoulders, his tapered waist. I could've counted the embroidered bones etched into the leather gloves that hugged his hands like they were dipped in ink.

There were so many options, but instead, I took the mortifying route. The slutty one. The one I'd never traveled down until now, chasing his scent away from my moral high ground.

Instead of doing any matter of socially acceptable things, I did the one thing that would probably get me punched.

I stared at his cock.

I was shocked, delighted, mortified, and *relieved* to find that it was hard. So *fucking* hard.

My mouth watered, my lashes fluttering as I eyed the thick swell of it. Though skeleton dude's voice was deceptively even, he was clearly just as affected by this. I could see the evidence of it right in front of me. I didn't fully understand what was happening between us, but that didn't stop me from leaning forward and closing the distance between my mouth and his dick. I'd never been the kind of guy that thirsted after anyone. Not even the fictional characters on TV—other than the occasional emaciated Victorian British boy. But, despite the fact it was totally out of character, I couldn't stop the way I nosed at the bulge in his surprisingly soft trousers with an eager whimper that, in any other situation, I would not have recognized as my own.

On the hunt for his missing scent, I nuzzled at the swell of his full balls, chasing the faint essence of him like a moth hunts a flame.

Finally, beneath the winter air, I caught what I'd been searching for.

On the surface, his essence was musky, *sweet*. Like graveyards and freshly turned dirt. Underneath that layer, I found a trace of the very real scent of sweat. I trailed it with my tongue, pressing flat against the now-slick fabric, desperate to taste. His cock twitched as I nosed at him, sucking eagerly as the cotton scraped the nerve endings on my tongue. Despite my enthusiasm, he didn't respond. Desperate for recognition, I pushed harder, sucking along the thick swell of his cock till I found where

his crown pressed tight against the fabric.

"Needy." Skeleton dude's voice was just as quiet, just as unaffected as before. Somehow, that only made me harder. *Slicker.* My hole clenched tight, and I doubled my efforts. Gloved fingers twisted in my hair, giving it a sharp tug that had me gasping as he forced my head back so he could look at me, my mouth still sucking at the now-damp fabric. "Greedy." His cock twitched, and I nearly howled my approval. "Sweet, *omega.*"

I'd never bought into the whole alpha-omega thing. Never been drawn to one before. Never wanted something the way I wanted now. This wasn't who I had been raised to be. But what I felt now was *different.* I was different. Like something about this encounter had rearranged who I was. A slut for dick. Like if I didn't get this large, thick—delicious cock inside me, I would die.

Through the mask, I could see his eyes were half-lidded. His lips curved upward, peeking beneath the teeth etched into the bottom of the skull, his skin painted with what looked like smudged charcoal to match bone and shadow.

"You want me," he said. Like it was that simple.

He'd asked me what I wanted.

I suppose he didn't need me to verbalize it to figure that out.

"Your name," I managed, muffled against the fabric. Somehow I couldn't force myself to release him, terrified of losing the already faint tease of his scent.

"You want my name?" he asked, amused. "Clearly you want a good deal more than that."

"Please." Wow. *Begging.* I'd never begged. Ever.

"Haden." His name rolled like silk from his tongue and I melted,

precum dripping down my crown as my hole gave a needy twitch. *Empty.* Haden.

"And yours?" Haden asked, his grip on my hair still tight enough my lashes fluttered from the sting.

"Percy?"

"Is that a question, Percy?" Amused again.

"Percy." I corrected myself, still nuzzling at his sac, chasing the scent of sweat like a starving man.

"You are *lovely*, Percy." Haden sounded almost reverent as he tightened his grip till my scalp tingled, and a gasp tore its way from my lips. "I did not know your people still offered sacrifices."

"They didn't. They don't." The words stumbled on my tongue before I could take them back. He was probably confused; hell, I was. I didn't know why I'd felt the need to correct him, only that for a moment the idea of him thinking my mouth on his dick was anything other than my own decision made me crazy.

"Why are you naked then, pet?" Again his fingers tightened till I answered. Pleasure-pain zinged down my spine and I gasped, my thighs trembling, my balls drawing up tight. If he did *that* again, I wasn't sure I would be able to stop myself from coming, so I distracted myself by answering his question.

"Money."

"Money?" Clearly my one-word answer wasn't enough because he stopped pulling my hair, and a needy, plaintive sound left my lips. I scrambled to answer again, desperate to be good for him. Desperate for him to hurt me again.

The feeling was so unlike me, it made my head spin.

I'd always run from pain, not chased it.

"I get free housing for the year if I can stay the night." It wasn't the whole story, but I didn't know how to explain the rest. It seemed cheap now, saying that out loud. Especially when, just moments prior, Haden had thought I was an actual human *fucking* sacrifice. But hell…it was the truth, and I'd never been any good at lying. My own honesty had gotten me into trouble more times than I could count.

"And this 'housing'…is important to you?" Haden clarified.

I thought about it.

Honestly, at that moment, no.

What was more important was getting through the layers of clothing separating my mouth from Haden's dick. I didn't say that, though. I was already acting like a whore, I didn't need to talk like one too. I could practically feel my mother rolling in her grave at the other side of the cemetery, and I shuddered, pushing that thought from my mind.

Hot, slick, wet-wet-wet.

My hole clenched around nothing.

Why weren't we fucking again?

Oh, right.

Because I was supposed to be answering Haden's question.

It was hard to remember what he'd asked, my mind was scrambled with images of me on my knees in the dirt, his cock in my mouth, gloved fingers stretching my ass wide. The fact I was a virgin had never meant I didn't have a wildly enthusiastic imagination. Saliva pooled on my tongue and I swallowed, sucking at Haden's heavy balls with renewed vigor. *C'mon fucker.* I could feel his cock twitch. *Don't let me down! Give in.*

"Did your…"

"Frat brothers?" I offered before greedily sucking again. Boo. He still wanted to talk.

"Did your 'frat brothers' know you were going into heat when they sent you here?"

Heat?

No.

No.

That couldn't be right.

I was on suppressants. Strong ones. Military grade. That wasn't possible. I hadn't had a heat since I was sixteen and my dad had locked me in the basement with a handful of pills and a water bottle.

No heat.

It couldn't be that.

"Not in heat," I said, though the words felt like ash on my tongue.

They felt like lies.

Haden made a soft, growly little noise that was equal parts frustrated and fond. He was a stranger and yet he still managed to be kinder to me than anyone had been in a long fucking time. My eyes burned as I shook my head, never straying far from where I'd made myself at home against his cock. "Can't be. Suppressants."

Words were harder to get out. Slippery as wet noodles.

"I hate to break this to you, darling, but you're wrong." He said it so easily, like stating my suppressants weren't working was a simple fact and not an earth-shattering problem.

Fear bubbled up inside me as my earlier visions of murderers and feral alphas came to mind again. I must've made a panicked noise because Haden hushed me softly, pulling my hair tight, just the way I liked, till I

relaxed again and resumed my needy nuzzling.

I tried not to think about how stupid I must look right now, lips swollen, eyes blown wide and dark.

Honestly, I wasn't sure I even cared.

Later, I would. I'd pick apart this encounter till all I had were bitter memories about myself, but for now, I was content to bask in his touch.

Heat.

I couldn't be in heat.

I couldn't.

I wasn't allowed.

"What are suppressants?" Haden asked, his voice curious, low. He had a strange way of speaking. Old-fashioned. Like he'd fallen right out of a storybook for overeager cock-sluts.

I didn't really want to answer, especially because alphas tended to be dicks when it came to omega birth control. They either went one of two ways: the traditionalists who believed omegas didn't have the right to make decisions about their own bodies, or the kind of alphas like my dad—the ones that thought omega was just a synonym for embarrassment. He'd been pumping me full of scent blockers and suppressants since the day I'd presented. My longest relationship was with two matching bottles full of little white pills. Dad had always put in every effort to stop the world from seeing that one of his boys had turned out wrong.

I'd never felt wrong until he'd told me I was.

I didn't know what kind of alpha Haden was.

I wasn't sure if I wanted to, if learning his nature would ruin the taste of him on my tongue, or the way I craved him inside my body.

"What are suppressants?" Haden asked again, endlessly patient.

Usually when people asked me questions multiple times, fists or anger got involved. Not now, though. But I was still conditioned to jump when I was told to—so I spoke, even though it was the last thing I wanted.

I just wanted him to touch me again.

"Suppressants make it so I don't go into heat. So that I don't feel the things the others feel. Block scents. Feelings. Whatever the fuck else."

"Why would you want that?" he asked, clearly curious.

Why *did* I want that?

I didn't know.

I couldn't remember.

Everything that had happened before seemed so very far away now. My skin was hot, my hole slick and empty as my fingers itched to do something—anything—to ease the ache of my rock-hard cock.

"I don't know," I said. Dumb, as always. "I'm just on them."

Haden made a noise, contemplative, like he was mulling over what I'd said. Clearly, I'd made a face or something because he asked, "Why does being off of them scare you so?" His fingers stroked through my hair, rubbing behind my ears till I mewled, then flinched, ashamed of the noise.

I'd never made *sounds* like this before. Breathy ones. Embarrassing ones.

Even jerking off was done silently, my teeth biting into my pillow, my sheets slick with cum.

"I have to be on them," I said again, because I didn't know what else to say—what he wanted me to say. But he didn't let it go. Huffing with anger, I glared at him.

I just wanted his dick, not a full-blown conversation.

"Why?" Haden asked again, nosy fucker.

I growled in frustration, eyes narrowed at him because this round of

twenty questions had scared away my irrational fear. Thinking was getting harder. So was my dick. Slick rubbed between my cheeks, dripping onto the ground, the chill winter air no longer creeping inside my bones.

The heat that burned inside me was too powerful even for a night as cold as this one.

"If I'm not on them, I don't…" Fuck. I didn't even know *what* would happen. The worst case scenario was pretty much my everyday reality. "Dad doesn't like it," I eventually settled on. That seemed the simplest way to explain it without diving into details.

"Your father forces you?"

"I don't know if I'd say *force*." Except, it was kinda true, wasn't it? Before Dad had chucked the pills at my head, I hadn't ever thought about it. Part of that was because I'd always just assumed I'd pop my knot at sixteen, like my brothers and my dad had. Hell, Dad was always raving about the fact that even Mom had been at least a beta. It was incredibly uncommon for an omega to be born into a family without one.

"If you are not being forced to take them and you dislike them, then why do it?"

Jee-sus.

Talk about beating a dead horse with a stick. (That was how that saying goes, right?)

"Jee-sus, dude. Just let me suck your dick." I had never in all my fucking life thought that I would say those words. *Ever.* And yet, here I was— panting for it, nuzzling against him, begging for a taste of the salty-sweet skin of his cock even though his questions made me want to smash my head against the nearest surface.

"You will touch me when I say you can touch me," Haden said.

I was dumb, so I didn't listen.

His pants didn't have a zipper, but they did have a row of shiny ivory buttons. In a surprising feat of dexterity, I flicked them all open in quick succession. He was wearing underwear. Boo.

Staring at the white trail of hair that led beneath the hem of his boxers, I had an out-of-body moment. My hands looked shaky and cold. My knuckles all fucked from the wind, chapped and dry. I was literally naked at the back of the fucking graveyard, thirsting after an actual demon-devil-thing's dick. What would happen if someone passed by and saw what I was about to do? Then again, that hadn't stopped me from getting naked and sitting here for four hours. So really, why would I let it stop me from getting fucked?

Priorities.

Haden made a noise, but it wasn't soft like the ones before. Playfulness disappeared as he pulled my hair tight, forcing my head back. Tingling all over, I realized he was being gentle before. This *hurt*. The good kind, and the bad. I gasped.

"If you want to touch me, you need to be obedient," Haden's words were a rumbled threat.

"Okay." I was stupid, not suicidal, so I agreed. Then there was silence as Haden scrutinized my face. His lips had pulled thin, his eyes glimmering with darkness as he traced them slowly down, down, down my body. My cock jumped.

"You want to be touched, yes?" Haden confirmed. He had this weird kind of voice. Rumbly, yet soft. Not too low. Not too high, either. Like it couldn't make up its mind. Like it was an illusion too—just like his shadows.

"Yes." Obviously.

"Have you been touched before?"

God, more talking. *When would it end?*

I didn't want to talk anymore, I was all talked out.

Obedient, I reminded myself. Or you won't get what you want.

"No." Even *I* knew I sounded petulant.

"Have you been fucked before?" The word "fuck" on Haden's cultured tongue sent a whirl of want through my body. Fuck sounded sinful when he said it. A word with a purpose. A promise.

"No."

"Do you desire to be fucked?"

"Oh, fuck yes." The way my voice wobbled—the words barely more than a gasp—gave away my enthusiasm. The heat inside my body was creeping closer to its peak. It wrapped me in honey from the inside, my limbs tingling, the need growing stronger with every labored breath.

Haden's scent wasn't enough anymore.

I needed to taste.

I needed to *feel.*

I needed—

I needed.

Haden released my hair. I didn't have more than a moment to mourn the loss because seconds later, his fingers were bumping against my lips as he tapped the leather and bone of his gloves against them, asking for entry.

Complying without a thought, I opened wide. Long fingers played with my lower lip for a moment, pulling it down, and releasing it with a soft *fwap.* Over and over he played until he grew bored and casually slipped his fingers inside my mouth. Haden traced over my teeth like he was

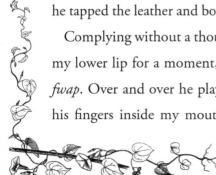

inspecting a new horse, before toying deeper to flirt with the slippery swell of my tongue.

The further he pushed into my mouth, the more right it felt. Something loose inside me clicked into place as I sucked, lax and obedient, letting him press a second finger inside. His gloves tasted like leather, butter soft on my tongue. It shouldn't have felt so good. He shouldn't have tasted like sin and sex, but he did.

As the second finger joined the first, I forced my jaw to stretch to accommodate their girth.

Drool slipped down my chin as I sucked with vigor, and Haden groaned, low and husky—the first real proof that he was just as affected by this as I was. The finger sucking felt like an audition and I was determined to be cast in whatever role he wanted me in, so long as I got a cock inside me at the end of the performance.

"You are a lovely surprise," he admitted. The sweet words were at odds with the brutal way he pulled his fingers out and shoved them back inside my mouth, the bone on top of his gloves gently clicking against my teeth. I whimpered. "Oh yes," Haden's voice grew deeper, throatier as he watched me suck. "You like this."

He was right.

I sucked again, slurping around the leather as he rubbed the back of my tongue just to watch my eyes water, then pulled out only to fuck inside again, harder.

Slurp, slick, slurp.

Staring at his face, I hunted for an expression behind the mask, but the shadow had swallowed him again. All I could see was a glimpse of hooded eyes and the way his lips were just slightly parted. His tongue was purple.

That *should've* alarmed me. Nearly lilac in color, it flickered out to wet his lower lip. I saw a glimpse of fangs and the base of my neck above my mating gland itched for something I couldn't bring myself to admit.

Then he distracted me again, pushing deeper—and deeper still.

By some miracle, I didn't choke, just held very, very still as Haden fucked me. It shouldn't have been as filthy as it was. It was just fingers. That was all. But the way they pressed inside me, I felt it all over my body. My hole clenched tight with need, my dick sloppy-wet as it bobbed and slapped my lower belly.

The deeper he pressed inside, the more I wanted.

"If you keep looking at me like that, I won't be able to hold back," Haden murmured, voice detached, though his fingers continued to slip in and out of me. Like he wasn't actively fucking me to tears.

My lips were pulled taut, my jaw a little sore. The bone on the top of his gloves gently caught my teeth. *Click, click.* I liked the sound. I liked how it felt, too.

Then his fingers left again and instead of shoving back inside like I expected, he let them trail wet across my cheek, tracing my jawline down to my throat where he swirled a circle of my own drool around my Adam's apple.

I shivered.

"Do you want me to hold back, Percy?" Haden whispered. "To be gentle?"

"No." I didn't recognize my own voice. It was too sweet. Too soft. Too *something.*

I watched enraptured as Haden stroked a gloved hand down his chest, tracing over the embroidered rib cage on his jacket, slipping down the knobs of stitched spine, till he reached the waistband of his underwear, black gloves stark against the pale lavender of his skin. He toyed just under the edge of the fabric, teasing me before swirling the curls of his bleached treasure trail playfully between his fingers. I nearly growled at him, jealous of the fact he got to play when I didn't.

Thankfully, it didn't take long before he grew impatient and shoved everything down and out of the way. The fat tip of his cock slapped against his lower abs and a smear of precum decorated the skin as he tugged his jacket upwards and I got a glimpse at more of his lovely purple belly. Other than being constructed from a monochromatic color palette, Haden wasn't much different from any other alpha I'd seen on my curious Google expeditions.

He was veiny and strong. His skin glistening with sweat, thick thighs spread as I watched his chest heave with each stuttered breath.

There was a jagged violet scar that bisected his abdomen and I wanted nothing more than to drown it with my tongue before sucking at the throbbing vein that danced up the underside of his gorgeous cock. It twitched hello before a drop of precum slipped down the uncut crown, and I salivated as I imagined what it would feel like to lean forward and taste.

Just a taste.

Just a little.

"Please," I whispered, staring at his cock with reverence. "I wanna know what you taste like."

"Darling," Haden murmured, reaching down with the hand he'd used to fuck my mouth, gathering the precum from his crown onto his thumb before he swiped it across my lower lip. I couldn't help the way my tongue flickered out eagerly, my lashes fluttering as the salty flavor lit up my body

from the inside out. I'd never so much as tried my own cum, despite my own curiosity, so the flavor was surprising. Not as bad as I'd expected. Kinda good, actually? In an animalistic sort of way.

More.

Leaning forward, I nuzzled at the soft lilac swell of Haden's sac. It was a darker color than his abs and throat, but not nearly as dark as his throbbing cock. The skin was velvety in texture, soft to the touch. Spongy hair rasped against my lips as I stared up at him reverently, waiting for his command.

"Suck."

I didn't need to be told twice.

Haden's dick was thick, thicker than I thought I'd be able to take. The fat crown dragged along my tongue as I took him inside my mouth, enthusiasm hopefully bridging the gap of inexperience. Yeah, okay. Damn. He tasted *good*, all sweet skin and musk. The scent of his sweat was deeper here, his natural perfume making my eyelashes flutter and my mating gland throb.

Haden grabbed my hair, squeezing it tight with his slick glove as he flexed forward and I took every inch he gave me without complaint. Every time I choked, he'd pull back just enough for me to catch my breath, before pressing back in again. Demanding. Commanding. Ruthless.

Everything I'd never known I wanted.

Even though I hadn't sucked dick before, I quickly got used to it, breathing through my nose, a regular old dick-sucking-champion. Even though I was pretty much a pro now I still choked when he pushed too deep, and part of me wondered if Haden did it on purpose because he liked to watch me struggle. Every time he pulled back and I caught my

breath, I could see the way his lips curled into a predatory smile.

"Good boy," he purred.

I should've been pissed but I wasn't. I just melted.

He liked the way I cried.

Which was weirdly flattering, and definitely hot as hell.

Tears streamed down my cheeks, drool slipping down my chin and throat as I labored with each ragged breath, my head bobbing between his spread legs. I couldn't tell if I was any good at this, or spectacularly horrible. But it was clear to me that neither of us were doing this purely to get off.

No.

There was something else there.

Like he wanted inside me just as much as I wanted him, pleasure be damned. An itch under our skin that could only be scratched with one another.

My hole twitched longingly, my dick so hard it was almost painful. I forced myself not to reach for it, though, because I didn't want him to stop. Didn't want to distract him from fucking my face. Somehow, I knew his demand for obedience extended to this as well.

Eventually though—maybe because I sucked at this, despite my earlier confidence—Haden pulled back.

His dick slapped against his belly, a wet little noise that made my cock jump and my toes curl in the dirt.

An owl hooted in the distance, but I ignored it, my face tipped up, lashes wet and cheeks streaked with tears.

"I'm going to fuck you," he said, fingers still gripping my hair. He didn't ask me. He *told* me. Like he already knew it was what I wanted.

"On your knees, chest to the ground, arch your back."

I quickly scrambled to comply.

Heat buzzed through my body, my head full of bees.

Getting into position was possibly the most awkward thing I'd ever done. No one else had ever looked at my ass like this before. All up close and personal. With dirt clinging to my knees and elbows I could feel Haden's eyes on my back, trailing down my spine, disappearing between my cheeks to where my hole was slick and empty.

I knew I had hair everywhere, and as my cheeks heated, I realized too late why most omegas shaved. This was intimate. Way fucking intimate. My thighs strained as I shuffled around, pressing my pecs to the cold ground as leaves crunched beneath my body and my cheeks burned with humiliation.

Did he *like* what he saw?

Probably not.

How could he?

I knew what I looked like.

Big. Muscular. Covered in cigarette burns. I wasn't the pretty omega, the one that got what he wanted. The one with the massive social circle, the lovely family, and many career prospects. I wasn't the kind of omega who had his pick of alphas, even if I'd wanted that. And I definitely wasn't the kind of omega who got his happily ever after.

I was just me.

Face down, ass up.

My hole, slick and wet and *aching*.

"These…suppressants," Haden began again, and I rolled my eyes heavenward in exasperation. I could feel his presence behind me, so

I clenched my jaw tight to keep from outwardly groaning. Weirdly enough, even though I didn't know *who* he was, or *what* he was, his figure looming at my back soothed me. My mating gland throbbed again. My dick leapt as his pants brushed against the back of my thighs. "Do they prevent pregnancy?"

"Can't get pregnant," I said, even though the words felt like ash in my mouth. There was a long, painful silence before Haden spoke again.

"Do you want this?" he confirmed, waiting for my answer.

Did I?

It seemed like a stupid question. Of course I did. I was the one that had asked for it in the first place. But then again…I arched my back, hoping that would be answer enough, but it wasn't. Because Haden didn't move.

"Fuck me." I'd never thought I'd say those words, but here I was. Here *we* were.

Me and…whatever the hell he was. Devil, demon, purple-fuckboy? Polite and shady—because shadows? (Ha!)

He slapped his cock gently against one of my ass cheeks and I groaned as a hot stripe of cum marked my flesh. Haden didn't ask for permission again. The same fingers that had been inside my mouth slipped leisurely down my crack, tracing around the twitching of my entrance till he gave it an almost perfunctory tap. My hole sucked needily at his fingers, but he didn't give in.

"You are just as greedy here as your mouth is."

I could hear his smile. Almost mean again. Sexy as all hell. His fingers gave another loose rub, and I clenched hard around nothing, the heat in my body making my tongue dry and my head thrum.

"Fuck me," I demanded again, more impatient.

"No." Haden murmured before one thick finger dipped barely a centimeter inside me. "Not until you beg."

Beg?

Fuck that. I'd already begged once today, I wasn't going to do it again. Demanding was more my style, apparently.

Except…as he slid deeper inside the hot clutch of my hole, everything I had ever known about myself slipped entirely from my head. His finger was almost cold because of the leather, slick and unyielding. A totally different sensation than a cock would be. Felt different than my own fingers, too. Better, honestly. They were longer and moved with single-minded purpose, reaching places I'd never been able to reach on my own. When he was all the way inside, I squeezed around him, letting him fuck me in that same detached way he'd fucked my mouth till my hole was sloppy and wet and he finally took pity on me, shoving a second finger inside.

I wasn't proud of the noise that escaped in response. Nor was I proud of the way I shoved back, eager to be fucked, genuinely grateful he hadn't played with my prostate yet because I knew the second he did, I was going to come all over my own sweaty chest.

Haden fucked like he spoke. Cultured. Confident. Playful.

Sometimes he slipped in quick and mean, sometimes he dragged out slow and sweet. The way he spread his fingers wide and watched my rim shudder, made me howl into the crumpled leaves beneath me. By the time he'd deemed me ready, my head was about to explode.

"Please," I begged, unable to recognize my own voice. Apparently, I'd forgotten my decision not to beg.

And then—fucking, finally—the thick head of his cock brushed my rim. It was hot, as hot as it had been inside my mouth.

For a moment, I desperately wished I could see it. See the tinged purple crown pop inside my body. Watch the way I swallowed him up, owning him the same way he owned me. I wished I could see him bite his lip, see the way his inverted eyes shuttered tight with pleasure.

"Perfect," Haden growled, kissing over my shoulder, his teeth and his mask catching on my sensitive skin as his cock slipped deeper inside me. It was thicker than his fingers. By a lot. And it kinda hurt at first—but in a way that was easy enough to ignore.

I knew what real pain felt like and this was...fuck. This wasn't *that*.

This was something else entirely.

Something new.

By the time his pelvis met my ass I was drooling all over myself again. He was big, bigger than me, that was for sure. I could feel his knot where it slapped against my rim as his hips gave short little thrusts to get me ready.

Perfect.

His words played on repeat in my mind as I shoved back, ignoring Haden's unspoken demand to let him take charge. It was that disobedience, however, that finally got me what I wanted.

Haden's teeth were surprisingly sharp when he bit me. He held the back of my neck tight, rendering me immobile as his cold gloved fingers grabbed my throat in one hand and his hips slapped hard against my ass. Without warning, he set a punishing pace that had me sobbing for mercy, tears slipping hot down my cheeks. The harder he fucked, the slicker I got, the wet sounds filling the air obscene.

My dick rubbed against my lower abs, aching and eager, and with each particularly brutal thrust it would slap against my belly in a way that made me tingle, a wet spot left behind.

"Shit," I gasped, body throbbing with pleasure. "Shit, shit, shit."

Haden shifted his hips, grabbing my ass tight in one massive hand as he moved me to change the angle. I trembled when he found what he was looking for, pushing up against something inside me that made my jaw drop open as a broken whine left my lips.

It was *so fucking good.*

Good enough that my eyes rolled back, my lashes fluttering as Haden's teeth dug in tighter, harder around my mating gland.

I should've been scared.

Even *I* knew what Haden was doing was considered impolite. If he broke skin, we'd be mated, and well…fuck. How the hell was I going to explain that? It was one of my worst fears, actually. Not because I didn't want it, but because I knew what getting it would mean for me.

Slap, slap, slap, his hips met my ass.

He gnawed at my neck.

My eyes rolled back with pleasure, despite the danger.

Haden didn't seem to care though, because his free hand slipped across my pelvis, dragging across my sweaty, sensitive skin till he reached his destination and squeezed tight around my throbbing dick. *Fuuuck.* That felt so fucking good. I humped into his grip, drunk on the way he panted behind me, hot breath caressing my neck. All thoughts of mating and its repercussions left my mind as the needy, desperate part of me that had been lurking under the surface since the moment I saw him broke free.

When he came, his fangs sank inside my neck.

The pain was so laced with pleasure I hardly noticed. The second I felt the heat of his cum inside me my own cock spurted across his fingers, balls drawing up tight as his knot popped inside me, and I distantly recognized that I was mewling.

Haden's teeth didn't release my neck as he forced me off my knees and onto my belly, letting me rest as his body bracketed my own and his cock released another shorter bout of his pleasure inside me. His clothing scraped against my sensitive skin, but I couldn't bring myself to care. Not when it felt so fucking good to be held down like this. To be overpowered, but protected. To not have to think or worry at all.

In a weird way, I felt...*powerful.*

That this large, frightening creature was mine until his knot popped free.

We were tied together and therefore vulnerable, but deep down, I knew Haden wouldn't let anything happen to me.

He would protect me.

Mate, my soul whispered as my lashes fluttered and I finally succumbed to sleep, his warm body atop my own.

Mate.

TWO

HADEN

Through smoke and shadows, he struggles toward me.
Like a phantom in search of light.
Sifting through fortresses and walls I constructed myself.
He stubbornly fights his way into my sight.

THREE

PERCY

The fact that the convenience store by my dorm building was only two hundred feet away should've meant the location was perfect. Except, standing between me and my deep-fried potato wedges and mini donuts was the highway that dissected the small town of Madison.

The only way to cross the busy street was to walk a mile down the road to the southern exit, smack the half-broken button, and cross the only crosswalk. Though some students—with a death wish—chose to jaywalk across three busy lanes and pray to the gods for mercy, I wasn't that kind of reckless.

I was feeling grouchy—not suicidal—so instead of braving the busy street, I wandered my way down the sidewalk, my headphones shoved in my ears. The fact that there was only one crosswalk was bullshit. The walk should've taken five minutes max but instead, it took a solid forty-five. Only the determined or truly stubborn still attempted it.

Which was apparently me.

I needed donuts.

Soda too.

Maybe a ring pop to suck on if I was feeling adventurous.

And fucking Tommy had taken my car to work, so I either had to wait for him to bring my car back—which I wasn't going to do because I wasn't a lazy piece of shit—or walk there myself.

Memories from my night in the cemetery a week ago spun to the forefront of my mind. Haden had been plaguing my thoughts constantly since the morning I'd woken up tucked safely beneath the bridge at the back of the graveyard, covered in dew droplets and a familiar black uniform jacket.

My mating bond was empty, even though I could still feel the throb of teeth and I'd chased Haden's scent in the fabric before ultimately deciding I needed to let go. It clearly hadn't taken, otherwise I would've felt him, right?

The jacket had been soft. Warm. A little small, when I tugged it on over my nakedness. But it worked well enough as I made the awkward waddling walk of shame with cum slipping down my thighs to where I'd stashed my clothes behind a grave a hundred or so feet away. As I had approached the familiar tombstone, I noticed that sitting on top lay a giant, dead grasshopper.

Poor thing.

I'd paused and debated the risk of staying out longer in the frigid-ass air as I got dressed in my usual t-shirt and ratty sweatpants, shoved my feet into my army boots, and ultimately decided to do the right thing, my cold-ass hands be damned.

With the grasshopper's fragile body cradled in my palms, I'd made my

way back to the bridge. There were too many rocks on the edge of the graveyard to dig him a hole there, and I didn't really want to wake up any angry spirits by digging in the grass above an already full grave. So, under the bridge we went to where the soil was soft and the trickle of a stream echoed from the other side.

I'd felt stupid and a little embarrassed by my own soft heart as I dug a hole in the ground one-handed, and held an admittedly shitty funeral for the deceased bug. The dirt had clung to my skin and the familiar sensation had grounded me, even though the silliness remained.

It felt familiar due to the countless hours I'd spent tending to the dirt at the greenhouse I worked at part-time.

Realistically, I knew the grasshopper probably didn't care whether or not it was buried. Hell, most critters didn't have funerals at all. Actually, none of them did, probably. (I'd have to Google that later.) I was pretty sure burying the dead was a human thing. So the funeral was probably more for me than the grasshopper.

But...

Thinking about leaving its body to rot in the wind?

Hell no.

Little dude deserved more dignity than that.

The jacket clinging to my shoulders continued to be suspiciously warm as I patted dirt over the no-longer-empty grave, rose to my feet, and squinted through the darkness to the other end of the bridge. Sunlight peeked beneath it, revealing nothing more than moss-covered boulders and fallen leaves.

No creatures, purple or otherwise.

No dudes parading as skeletons.

35

If my ass hadn't been absolutely reamed the night before, I probably would've thought I had imagined the whole thing. But I could still feel the stretch of Haden's knot, a phantom pleasure that had my hole clenching and my neck throbbing where he'd bitten me.

And that was a whole other thing, wasn't it? The fact that he'd fucking bitten me at all. *Who did that?* What a dickbag. Especially since whatever pseudo-heat had started the night before had apparently fled with the first beams of sunlight. My pills had decided to magically work again this morning because the air was just as stale and dead as it usually was. Haden's scent was almost entirely gone, despite the fact that I still had his cum leaking out of my ass.

A bite and run.

Asshole.

I hadn't known what to do.

So I glared into the darkness, raised my dirt-covered hand, and flipped off the shadows. When that didn't make me feel any better, my stolen jacket and I had plodded unhappily back toward the parking lot to forget the night before and take a much needed shower.

I figured the least Haden could do was let me keep his fucking jacket since he got to keep my virginity.

The only thing that had kept me sane was the fact that despite the scar on the back of my neck, the bond hadn't seemed to take. I was more sure of that as time passed without the telltale ache of longing for a partner I wasn't even sure was human.

But *that* had been a week ago.

And now, I was here crossing the highway as the bitter wind bit at my cheeks, wondering why the hell I couldn't seem to forget that night. In

my dreams, I hunted for the memories, unable to stop. And unable to forget the fact that Haden's jacket was shoved under my bed, hidden inside a box for safe-keeping. I didn't want Tommy to see it and ask where I'd gotten it.

He'd take one look at it and either rib me for answers, or try to steal the damn thing. I wasn't a fashion expert, but even I could tell it was pretty magical. In the light of day, I'd taken it out more than once to admire the swirling embroidery, and to chide myself for stupidly believing in magic at all. I'd spent too long tracing over the frankly realistic bones till I had their shapes memorized before I'd guiltily shoved it back into the box and tried to forget about it all over again.

The ribcage embroidery was particularly gorgeous.

Which wasn't something I'd thought I'd ever say, so yeah.

Apparently, I was full of surprises lately.

By the time I reached the convenience store, I was huffing and puffing and my lungs were frozen stiff. I bought my donuts, a soda, and a pack of Cheez-Its with a nod to my favorite cashier before I sat down on the curb out front to stuff my face, trying to forget the dreams that had haunted me since the night I'd spent in the graveyard.

I shoved three donuts in my mouth at once, my flashcards in my other hand as I glared out at the highway. It pissed me off to watch the cars that zoomed by, seemingly without a care in the world. I only wished I was that carefree. I was a scholarship student, despite being stupid, so grades mattered. Which was why I was studying for a test in my least favorite class by inhaling my scribbled notes with my eyeballs one-handed while stuffing my face with the other.

Every moment mattered when it came to my schooling. I hadn't

decided on a major yet, but my counselor assured me there was still time.

Dad didn't think I'd make it here.

Hell, I hadn't thought I could either.

But here I was. It had been a year and a half and somehow—miraculously—I hadn't flunked out yet. In fact, I was pretty much enjoying it. I liked the schedules. I liked learning. Most of all, I liked being far, far away from home. The greenhouse I worked at on campus had become my safe space the second I'd stepped inside it. So, without college—without the boring as hell classes—I wouldn't have found my favorite plot at the back of the garden.

The money helped too, even though working part-time didn't really pay much.

I was grateful.

Although, it often felt like my brain was about to bleed out my ears.

I finished my donuts in silence and moved on to my crackers, stuffing my cheeks full like a chipmunk as my saliva did half the work, my fingers smudging salt on my index cards. Jesus. Had I been high when I wrote half of these? I didn't think so. But they didn't make any fucking sense.

I mourned the fact that studying at college meant, well...*studying*.

A horn blared and without looking up, I tore my Cheez-It-delivering hand out of the bag and flipped off the oncoming vehicle. Stupid of me, sure. It could've been someone bigger than me, stronger too—but I was more scared of flunking out of school than I was of some territorial asshole in the middle of a public parking lot.

The horn blared again.

Jee-sus.

I rolled my eyes and raised my head, ready to tell whoever was

interrupting me to fuck off, only to stop short when I realized I was looking at my own fucking car.

"Get in." Tommy's familiar head was shoved out the driver's side window and his shit-eating grin ate up the delicate real estate of his face. I didn't argue, used to taking orders from him and everyone else. Instead, I just shoved my cards back in my hoodie pocket along with my soda and half-eaten crackers, then chucked my donut wrappers in the trash.

It was warm inside the car. Warm enough that it made me realize just how cold I'd gotten on my walk over.

I cranked up the heat and reclined my seat, chewing on my lip as I waited to hear what sort of nonsense Tommy was about to spew.

Tommy knew everything about everyone, ever.

And that wasn't even an exaggeration.

"How was work?" I asked after a few tense seconds, when it was clear that the other omega wasn't about to speak.

"Same old, same old." He was subdued. Which was entirely unlike him.

I turned to look at him for probably the first time since that night. I knew it would be hard to dodge his questions, so I'd spent the majority of the week avoiding him. I didn't really want him knowing my business. And I knew it was only a matter of time before he asked about the massive bandage I had pasted to the back of my neck. This was the first time we'd really talked since I'd showered off Haden's scent, went to the store, and splurged on turtlenecks. The bite had healed quicker than it should've, but I hadn't known what else to do to cover it up.

Having a mating bite made me a red fucking flag. I couldn't claim to be beta walking around with an alpha's mark on my skin.

I could count on one hand the number of people that knew I was an

omega, and I wasn't ready for that number to expand. Fuck, I didn't even *want* to know what my dad would say—what he'd think—what he'd *do* to me if he found out I'd rolled over and presented my ass like a bitch in heat. His reactions were always over the top, and his rage sometimes blinded him, even though realistically, I knew a bitch in heat was kinda what I was. Not that I'd ever say that to him.

I knew there was no shame in being an omega.

I *knew* that.

I looked at guys like Tommy—who were all smiles. Pretty. Small-framed. Whip smart, and full of charisma, and I knew, deep down, for omegas like him being what we were could only be a blessing. But for me? Fuck no.

That's why I'd been avoiding him.

He wouldn't get it.

He couldn't.

We weren't the same, even if we were.

"How did you know where I was?" I asked, trying to break the silence. My soda sat heavy where it stretched the limits of my pocket, and I shifted uncomfortably on the worn leather seat. I'd had to duct tape the edges last summer when they'd finally popped free, but otherwise good old Bessy—my Honda Civic—was in pretty damn good shape considering how old she was, and how many owner's she'd had before I came along.

Most would call her junk.

I called her my best girl.

"Wasn't hard to figure it out," Tommy told me with a huff. "When you avoid me, you always go stuff your face somewhere, and I already checked the cafe on campus and you weren't there."

I wanted to argue but he was right. About both things. "You noticed?"

"Course I fucking noticed, Percy."

I could feel Tommy's glare and I shrank in my seat, attempting to make myself smaller even though that wasn't physically possible.

"You didn't watch *The Terminator* with me even though we had it planned for like over a month. You leave the room whenever I enter it—and you've got this shifty look on your face—like always." He sniffed. "I don't know what I did to offend you, but the least you could do is tell it to my face."

That was one thing I liked about Tommy.

He didn't beat around the bush. In some ways, he was more straightforward than my brothers—or even I was. Even though he admittedly had a lot more complicated emotions.

Maybe I was being stupid by keeping what had happened from him.

Maybe.

But that night had felt like a dream and I wasn't sure whether or not it was a nightmare yet.

My neck throbbed with the memory, and without thinking, I reached up and rubbed the sore bond bite.

Tommy's gaze immediately snapped to where I was rubbing, and his eyebrows flew up comically fast.

"Turtlenecks," he said, realization dawning. "Turtlenecks!" He slapped his hands on the steering wheel and his eyes narrowed as he stared me down. "Um. Percy? Please tell me that's not a bond bite you're hiding."

I grimaced because I knew I'd done this to myself. Stupid. If I'd just… not touched it, he wouldn't have noticed. God. Now I had to explain what happened? Or maybe…maybe I could *lie*.

Except, I knew I was a shit liar.

But *maybe* I could make this work anyway.

"Some asshole bit me. That's why I've been avoiding you." A half-truth. Enough that I could see the way Tommy's green eyes lit up with evil glee and revenge began to brew behind them as surely as I'd known it would.

"Who was it? I'll chop his balls off."

Ew.

I thought about Haden's lovely purple balls. Then I thought about them chopped off. And my whole face scrunched up with disgust. "No, thanks."

"*Seriously.*" He took a left toward the dorm a little too abruptly and I had to cling to the door frame for much needed support. I really shouldn't let him drive my car considering what I knew about his driving abilities. But he always asked so nicely...and I was a sucker for those big green eyes.

"I said no thanks."

"Just give me a letter." Tommy parked the car with a lurch and I almost lost my lunch, sagging a little when we were safely under our numbered awning as he pulled the keys from the ignition. He chucked them at me, and I caught them with a glare. "Just the first letter of his name, that's all I'm asking."

I debated with myself.

I wanted to say no because he was almost as much of a nosy fucker as Haden was.

But...Tommy would keep pushing. He never knew when to fucking quit. Annnnd he was my best friend. So really, what was the harm of one simple little letter?

If I actually *had* been bitten by someone on campus, a letter was all

42

Tommy needed to hunt the prick down like he so obviously wanted to. He thought I couldn't see behind his sneaky little smile, but I could see the evil lurking under his glittery innocent gaze. It was why I liked him so much, after all.

He was as loyal as a rabid chihuahua guarding the fridge.

"Fine." There wasn't any way he'd find Haden. Hell. I wasn't even sure he really existed. Aside from the jacket and the bite, there was nothing to prove it. But…I didn't really want Tommy mad at me. I *had* missed our movie night…so I acquiesced. "H."

"H." Tommy hummed thoughtfully, slipping out of the car with a flourish and slamming the door shut. I inhaled with a huff, chasing a scent I knew I wouldn't be able to smell, ignoring his grin because it wasn't settling me like it normally did. He rapped on the window and I got out of the car, stomping my way toward the stairs.

Man.

Haden wasn't even fully real and he was still messing me up.

With a shake of my head, I headed up the steps to the main entrance. The giant symbol etched above the door laughed at me as I passed beneath it. This was the omega dorm, and all you had to do was see the designation sign to know it. I did my best to duck through the side door when I came on my own, to avoid people seeing me, but that wasn't an option when Tommy was with me. Always felt like a lie coming here. Or maybe…not a lie? But…wrong.

It just felt wrong.

I didn't belong here.

That's why I'd applied for the frat in the first place. The guys liked me well enough. They invited me to their parties—they greeted me in class.

When it was football season, I got more back slaps and ass taps than usual as they passed by me on campus since I'd enjoyed more than a few practice matches last summer. Every fundraiser, every party, every match I was there.

They *liked* me.

I fit in with their dirty socks, big shoulders, and friendly manly camaraderie. Reminded me of being home, what it had felt like being the youngest of three brothers. Passed between rough hands like a shiny new toy only to be discarded when I stopped crying quite so much.

"Did you hear back from the dick-o-saurs?" Tommy asked as we headed up the staircase.

I knew who he meant.

The same guys I called my friends Tommy privately referred to with a variety of colorful insults. Even though I did like our spa nights, and the fact that he had a black belt in MMA, he didn't *get* it. Didn't get why I needed them the way I did. As much as I liked Tommy, he wasn't…what I knew.

And that was scary.

"I get to move in at the beginning of next semester," I admitted, cheeks a little hot. All the paperwork was done now, everything set in stone. This was a sore spot between us. Tommy didn't want me to move out. He claimed it was because he'd miss me, but we both knew it was because he didn't think I could make it out there on my own, which was why I was determined to prove him wrong, even though he was probably right.

Tommy's voice in my head called me a pessimist again, and I mentally flipped him off.

"Are you gonna tell your dad?" the real Tommy asked.

That was a loaded question.

Dad didn't know I was living in the omega dorm in the first place. If he did, he wouldn't have let me go to college at all. I swallowed the lump in my throat as I forced myself to speak.

"He probably won't ever visit." I hoped anyway. That would be a cluster fuck. Despite only being a forty-minute drive from home, none of my family had ever visited me during the entire year and a half I'd been attending college in Madison.

I didn't mind though, honestly.

The little mountain town had become precious to me. Like a well-guarded secret. I coveted the old brick buildings, the chipped sidewalks, and the hungover students waltzing around campus. I wasn't sure what would happen if my family came, but if my two worlds collided, I didn't think I could survive the aftermath.

Didn't want to hear my brother's laughter here, or witness my father's silent disapproval. Beneath it always sat a darker anger, simmering under the surface. I didn't like when I brought it out of him and I knew my "sissy little garden" and my "pansy friend" would make him boil over.

Tommy just shook his head at me, but he didn't push again as he shoved open our bedroom door, waited for me to enter, then flopped down on his bed with a dramatic sigh.

"Terminator?" he offered hopefully, even though he'd already watched it without me, his dark hair flopping all over before he pushed it back out of the way.

I thought about my index cards and the fact that I'd only gone through half of them.

But then Tommy gave me his puppy dog eyes, and I sighed, already

calculating how late I'd have to stay up to catch up while he slept. "Okay, but you're gonna get the popcorn."

Maybe if I was tired enough, I could stop searching for Haden in my sleep.

"You already have snacks," he pointed out.

"I'm not sharing." I guarded my full hoodie pocket, eyes narrowed.

Kids who grew up with everything didn't understand what it was like to hunt for scraps in the back of barren cupboards. So no. I wasn't going to share. He could buy his own fucking Cheez-Its.

"Fine, fine. Be stingy." Tommy obviously didn't care that much because he just grinned at me as he hopped to his feet again and fled toward the bedroom door. "I'll be back in a jiffy."

"Sure."

The door shut with an audible click and I sighed, scrubbing my hands up over my face as I glared around our familiar room. Tommy's side was covered in *Clueless* and Cary Grant posters. All his toiletries and his spa kit were stacked together neatly in rows inside a cabinet he'd brought from home when he moved in. I'd miss this place when I was gone. Miss him too, even though he plagued me with the scent of acetone three days a week. Acetone just so happened to be one of the scents I could still fucking smell, lucky me.

But I'd miss that too. This room had been my first home away from home. My ratty old blanket was folded neatly across my bed, the same pillowcase I'd had since I was ten and obsessed with *Toy Story* decorating my decade-old pillow. Mom had bought it for me at Target for my birthday and every time I looked at Woody's happy stupid face, it made me smile.

Everything I'd contributed to the room was covered in holes. Hand-me-downs. Keepsakes. Precious.

Tommy's side of the room, however, was all new shiny things that came in plastic wrap and had a price tag long enough that if I tried to read it my eyes would cross.

We were so different and yet somehow, worked so well.

I'd miss him so much when I was gone. I knew realistically we could still be friends. But it would take more effort on his end, and honestly, I wasn't sure I was worth that. Hell, no one else had made the effort before.

The thought unsettled me, so I shoved it away, staring at my bed as the tease of what I hid beneath it came to mind.

I wanted to get Haden's jacket out again, to search for comfort in his scent like I'd been shamefully allowing myself to do all week, but I forced myself to sit on my hands instead, my soda a heavy lump in my pocket. I didn't have time. Tommy would be back soon. I'd barely gotten out of the last conversation with Tommy unscathed, the last thing I needed was more scrutiny.

Plus, I didn't want to share Haden, whatever small bits of him I still had.

Despite this, I missed his scent all the same.

Even when Tommy returned with a giant bin of buttered popcorn and a hopeful skip in his step, I missed him.

Haden's jacket sat under the bed, mocking me.

Soothing me.

Taunting me with something I could never have.

FOUR

PERCY

I didn't make friends. Couldn't, really. I'd always been shit at small talk, and as much as I'd craved companionship, I hadn't wanted to subject anyone else to my family. So that was why at first it hadn't occurred to me that Tommy and I could ever be anything at all other than roommates. It wasn't how I was wired. Growing up as I had, surrounded by my dad and his friends, my brothers and theirs, there hadn't been an opportunity to meet someone like Tommy before.

It had been my first day on campus. Flowers were popping through their beds and birds flitted from branch to leafy-green branch as our group headed toward the science building. We'd been touring campus all morning, working our way south in a gaggle of freshmen, and I'd heard a noise behind me before turning to investigate. That's when I saw him.

Tommy was laughing in the center of a squad of people of all shapes and sizes—though he hadn't been Tommy to me then—just a brunet omega with a pointy chin and purple Doc Martins. His head was tossed

back, his green eyes crinkled. The others flocked around him, soaking up his laughter and I just stared and *stared* at him. Because he was everything I would never be, walking around like he didn't realize how lucky he was.

Lithe, beautiful, loud, and free.

I should've hated him.

But I didn't.

Instead, I found myself gravitating toward him. Like a cat basking in puddles of sunshine on a warm spring day. I soaked him up like sunbeams because I knew if I couldn't be him, the least I could do was watch him be.

I'd never been more shocked than the day I walked into my dorm room and realized Tommy was going to be my roommate. Imagine my surprise when we rarely argued. At least, most of the time.

Now we were butting heads a bit.

"Look, Percy, I get that you don't want your dad to know where you've been staying, but I draw the line here."

"Where?" I stopped folding my clothes, my hands shaking a little as my shoulders drew up tight and I glared down at a pair of my holey mismatched socks. I chucked them to the side, my movements jerky. I hated when he got like this, all agitated. Made me wanna bare my teeth and run. I'd known this confrontation was coming, but the inevitable fight still made my hackles rise.

Tommy had been side-eyeing me for days now. The closer we got to my move in at the Alpha Beta Phi house, the more tense our conversations had become. Clearly, he thought I was being stupid, though I didn't really get why.

He was about to tell me, though.

I could taste his anger in the air.

Bitter, sharp.

"You can't keep living like this. It would be different if he was like…I don't know, some distant uncle or whatever, and didn't know your designation—but fuck, dude. He's your dad. And you're an *omega*. He knows you are. He's *always* known. You—*and he*—can't change that fact."

He'd probably rehearsed that. It *sounded* rehearsed. I could feel my blood thrumming the way it always did when I was under attack, though this time I knew not to expect anything physical. That wasn't Tommy's way. He was a guy, but he wasn't *that* kinda guy.

I didn't know what to do with him sometimes.

He was all talk, talk, talk. Like talking ever solved anything.

Newsflash, it didn't.

All it got you was two black eyes and a sore jaw.

"I know it's hard for you to accept—even though you are stubborn as fuck and won't tell me why—but I'm not blind. I don't need you to tell me with words that the only reason you're leaving is because you're terrified of what your dad will do when he finds out you disobeyed him."

Fuck, I never should've drunk tequila with him last month. He wouldn't have known shit if I hadn't gotten weak one night after visiting home and spewed my secrets—and my insides—all over our shared bathroom floor.

I never drank, for good reason.

It only ever led to trouble, especially for a lightweight like me. The fact that Tommy could drink me under a table despite being half my size was just another fuck you from the universe.

"It's not that." I was quick on my feet, dodging the question because that was what I'd always done. It was the way of things. Take a few

punches to appease, then dodge when the going gets too rough and the attacker has finally tired themselves out.

"If it's not that, then what is it?"

I didn't have an answer for him. Truthfully, I didn't even have one for myself. Deep down I knew Tommy was right, but I refused to admit it. It was one thing to spill secrets when your blood was pumping with tequila and something else entirely to do so stone cold sober while folding threadbare socks. My silence only incensed him, though.

"Do you really want to live with a bunch of alpha-holes?" *No. I really didn't.* "The stench alone should dissuade you."

I rolled my eyes.

Tommy didn't get me. Didn't get the way the smell was faint, but familiar. He was always going on and on about sweaty socks and man feet. When he said it like *that*, yeah, it was pretty gross. But it kinda smelled like home there, however weakly my nose was able to pick it up. Scent blockers made it so I couldn't smell the distinct alpha scents anyway, so I didn't get why he thought it was such a big deal.

"What if you want to get off scent blockers and suppressants?" He asked for like the millionth time. "If you're in an alpha house pretending to be a beta, you literally can't. You're committing to two or more years of ingesting literal poison."

"It's not that bad."

"It is if you never fucking take breaks, Percy. I know you say you had a heat before starting college, but that's just not enough."

I could hear how angry he was without having to turn around and see his red face. I wondered how mad he'd be if I admitted I'd lied about that particular piece of information.

51

I hadn't had a heat since I'd turned sixteen, not that I'd tell *him* that. Judgey-McJudgerton that he was.

"You don't *want* to do this, Percy," Tommy insisted.

"I do." It was like he wasn't even listening. Or maybe his comments were hitting too close to home. Either way, anger tingled inside me as my hands began to shake.

"No, you don't. *You don't.* You just want to please your dad."

Alright. *Now* I was officially done with the conversation.

"I'm officially done with this conversation," I repeated out loud, shoving my laundry aside as I turned around to glare at Tommy. He was standing just like I'd thought he'd be, legs spread, his hands on his hips. His stupid purple boots that I kinda love-hated were tumbled haphazardly half under his bed.

"Percy—"

"I'm serious, Tommy. Fuck off." I glared at him, my temper erupting as I stomped my way to our shared coat rack and tore my jacket from it. My movements were jerky and uncoordinated as I put it on and then shoved my way out into the hallway, Tommy's words still ringing in my ears.

I found myself at the graveyard.

Again.

It was just as cold out as before, and I idled in my car for a whole five minutes before I decided to say fuck it and head toward what I'd privately dubbed Haden's bridge. Maybe he was the devil from the stories—maybe he wasn't. But his memory had been haunting my dreams for weeks now and I figured the least he could do was suffer through my black mood with me.

My unfinished bond was quiet as I approached, stepping around graves out of politeness, my worn hand-me-down army boots crunching on the still-dry, fallen leaves. It hadn't snowed yet. But there was still time.

Winters in this part of the north were always full of dry wind and blistering cold, even after the first snow had fallen. It was pretty though, even if it was uncomfortable.

When I found the grasshopper grave I'd dug, I sat beside it, soaking up the darkness beneath the bridge, listening to the drip, drip of water droplets as they made their way to the cobblestones.

"Why'd you bite me?" I asked the quiet, because it was something that had been bothering me since that night.

I'd searched my dreams for answers, but all I'd gotten were glimpses of the alpha who had left me behind. In the bath. Eating dinner. Sitting alone in the dark. Peeks at a future that didn't exist, a world that wasn't real, a man that didn't want me. "Why do it, if you didn't know what it meant?"

Maybe that wasn't it though. Maybe he'd known. Maybe he just hadn't cared about the very real repercussions his bite would instill upon me. "I was never gonna mate anyways," I told the dark, my heart in my throat, "but if my dad sees he'll—" The words choked on the way out so I shoved them back inside me, keeping them safe in the gaping hole where my heart lay dormant.

"Whatever." I snorted to myself, kicking at a rock, careful to rearrange the makeshift cross I'd laid across the grasshopper grave so it was upright once again. Stupid because the grasshopper didn't give a shit. But I had to do it anyway.

I sat there for a long time.

Long enough I had ignored at least seven of Tommy's buzzing phone calls. Long enough the sun had set and the bitter cold had swept in once again. Finally, I rose to my feet and made my way back through the graveyard toward where I'd parked, my anger gone, Tommy forgiven.

I didn't have any more answers.

And somehow, I knew Haden would be visiting my dreams again that night, and I didn't know how to feel about that.

FIVE

HADEN

*N*o matter where I hide, he finds me.
    Sunlight is not something I knew I could yearn.
He chases me though I've turned the lights off.
There is no darkness he leaves unturned.
And I am forced to welcome him.
Lest I be the last shadow burned.

SIX

PERCY

"You're back again," Haden's voice echoed through the quiet, and I startled, shifting around till my eyes adjusted to the dark and I could make out his shadowy figure in the corner of what looked like...a library? The vague scattering shapes of bookshelves lined the walls, and pillars dipped in indigo so dark it was nearly black rose toward the ceiling to support a glass dome that bled red instead of blue like a starry night sky should.

It took me longer than it should've to reply to him.

This was a dream, after all. Wasn't it?

He could wait for me. He had no choice.

Still though, I didn't want to be a total dick, so instead of admiring the mahogany desk Haden sat behind or the piles of books that toppled like ancient buildings stacked along the floor, I turned to him.

"Back?" I asked because I wasn't sure what he meant.

Sure, I'd been dreaming of him for weeks, dreaming of this place.

But it had always felt murky at best, the details foggy, like I was stretching, stretching, stretching toward something and never quite reaching it. Like there was a veil between me and what lay before me, thick as molasses, waiting for my fingers to rip it to ribbons so I could push my body through.

"You've been here before," Haden stated plainly. I blinked.

"Is this…a place?" I gestured around me, encompassing all of the dream with curiosity I probably shouldn't have had. But he made me curious, and I couldn't help that fact.

"It is a place, among other things." Haden didn't rise from his seat and as my eyes adjusted more, I noted he was back in his skeleton garb again. What lay beyond his skull mask was nothing but mystery, though his lips looked soft, yet stern. A longing flickered in my chest that I swiftly rubbed away.

Maybe this dream was actually a nightmare.

Something I'd conjured up to punish myself for giving in all those nights ago.

"I didn't know your people possessed magic such as this," Haden added, his own voice curious now. Obviously, I was an enigma to him. Our first encounter had gone much the same way. A lot of "I didn't know your people did this, and that." A lot of wonder and trepidation aching through the rippling tones of his voice.

"Magic?" I scoffed. "I'm not magic."

"I beg to differ."

Cute, but weird.

Was he flirting?

Did that mean I was flirting with myself?

"Where are we?" I asked because I wanted to interrupt my own annoying thought process. Also, because I was curious. Curious, like he was.

"My office."

Well, that was obvious.

I glared at him.

"Your office?" I glanced around, scanning the piles of books, the littered paper, the wall sconces that should've been lit, but instead, were as dry and dead as old bones. Dubious, I narrowed my eyes on him again. "Why are you at an *office*? What are you?" I folded my arms. "You don't look like an office drone." Not that this looked like your typical office drone's office. Oh no. I wasn't sure what this looked like.

A dungeon maybe?

A dungeon if it had banged a library, and this was its very dark, very gothic baby.

"I assure you, an office drone I am not."

I stared at Haden for a long moment, waiting for him to continue, but he didn't. He just shuffled the papers on his desk, his head tipped down. I hadn't noticed before, but his hair was shorn close to his scalp. An almost military style haircut that perfectly matched the uniform he obviously had a whole closet full of. The hair was pearly white all over and looked soft as puppy fluff, though there was a curious stripe of black that ran from his hairline all the way to the back, almost like a reverse skunk stripe.

I'd yelled at a skunk once.

Not because I wanted to.

I'd been feeding him scraps at the edge of the trailer park for months and when Dad caught wind of it, he'd made me scare him off. The look on his little face, so confused by my betrayal, still haunted me.

That was the last time I'd cried. You had to do what you had to do to survive in my house growing up and sometimes that meant others getting hurt. My heart still tore when I thought about it. I rubbed the spot where it ached as I turned my attention away from Haden's hair and took a cautious step forward.

He couldn't hurt me, right? Not if this was my dream.

Except I'd had dreams where I got hurt before, so that logic wasn't exactly sound.

Haden spoke before I could tunnel myself into an even darker anxiety spiral. "How long are you staying this time?" His voice was wary, though curious as I continued to shuffle and stare at him, my hands shoved into my armpits, shoulders drawn up high and tight.

"I don't know." What the hell did that mean? It wasn't like I'd come here on purpose. I couldn't really leave when I wanted to. *If* I wanted to. Which I didn't. This was a definite improvement compared to my life when I was awake.

There weren't alphas like this at home.

Or…books? Yeah. *Books.* The books were cool too.

The alphas were better, though.

"Fine." He sighed, then shuffled his paperwork around, shoved it to the side and folded his hands across the glistening table top. More details of the room came into focus. The engravings along the edge of the desk, a little skeleton army marching forever onward. The dripping candles, with wax that had long since dried, their wicks and lives burning out in tandem.

I was nervous.

I fidgeted a little, waiting for him to speak, because somehow my words had dried up.

This reminded me too much of feelings I had long tried to bury. Of childhoods built on broken promises, crumbling foundations, and rationed laughter.

The uncertainty should've been familiar. I should've soaked it up like I normally did when I chased things that were bad for me. But it didn't. Maybe that meant Haden wasn't truly bad? Or maybe that meant the moral compass I possessed had finally gone and broken.

"You look frightened, pup." Haden rose from his seat and edged toward me. It was almost like a mating dance. He was a big colorful purple bird, fluffing his feathers, or in this case, his bones toward me. My bond mark throbbed, my legs stiff and numb as I shuffled back a pace, and then forced myself to still. I didn't want to look weak. Didn't want to look frightened. Being scared had never won me anything.

The closer Haden got, the more I trembled. Like there was electricity between us, zapping at my fingers, my toes, my everything till I was zip-zip-zipping away, ready to combust, my hair standing on end.

When he was close enough that I could scent him, something inside me quivered. I squashed it quickly, keeping my expression as unreadable as I could, my jaw tensed, my lips drawn thin. And then…his fingers were touching me. He didn't have gloves on this time, and his skin was molten hot. He traced over the swell of my cheek bone and something inside me ignited.

"Do you think I want to hurt you?" Haden's words caressed the shell of my ear, detached almost, but…underneath all that ice was curiosity. Like a creature that was just waking up.

"I don't know," I answered honestly. "Do you?"

I could never fucking tell.

"If I wanted to hurt you, you would not be standing here, looking up at me so prettily."

I wanted to point out that I was thicker than him, even if he was tall, but I bit my tongue, my heart wobbling as my traitorous pulse thrummed, pretty, pretty, *pretty*. No one called me pretty. Except Haden, apparently. I wasn't sure if he was blind or lying, but I wasn't about to argue.

Then the other half of his words hit, and I relaxed, some of the tension bleeding away as I realized he was right. If he wanted to hurt me, he'd already had ample opportunity. Instead, all he'd done was approach me like I was a wild raccoon and his words were kitchen scraps.

I lapped them up like the greedy little trash panda I was.

Swallowing the lump in my throat, I said, "So why am I here then?"

"That I cannot answer you."

That night came back to me. The cold. The bite of hot fingers. His knot. His cock. His...*rejection*. His abandonment. Waking up alone with only dew drops and dead grasshoppers for company. "Why..." I trailed off.

"Hmm?" Haden's fingers stroked my cheek again, and I shuddered, melting.

"Why did you bite me?" I blurted out, the thought having occurred to me suddenly. It had been bothering me since that night, the loss and anger bubbling up beside the hurt all over again as I recalled this wasn't the first time he'd called me pretty. "Why bond with me when you knew you were going to leave? When you knew it wouldn't take?"

Now I wasn't so sure about that last bit, since the second I'd seen him again, the mating mark on my neck lit up in a happy little tap dance, endorphins bubbling up inside me as I trembled and my scent-blind nose chased Haden's sultry essence.

"Didn't I?" Haden stroked my cheek again, his words so quiet it was almost like he was speaking to himself. He sounded a bit confused, maybe…amazed? I tipped into the touch, unable to help myself. No one touched me like this. Ever. "If the bond had not taken, I don't think we would be talking right now."

I supposed that made sense.

But it didn't answer why he'd done it.

"But, why bite me at all?"

Haden's fingers paused as he mulled over his words. I watched the way his lips pressed together, chasing his eyes inside the shadows of his mask, though in this light they were nearly impossible to see. Just fathomless dark depths. "Truthfully, I did not remember the significance."

What was that supposed to mean?

"You're an alpha. How could you not remember what a bond bite is?" God, either this guy was dumb or he thought I was.

Maybe he was right, because he started stroking again and I ate that shit up right away, practically purring.

"I am many things," Haden explained softly. His fingers never ventured. Only petted away, lighting up little fires in their wake as he traced along my temple, toying with the soft brunet flop of bangs I religiously gelled out of my face. "I have not been an alpha for a very long time."

"I don't get it." I glared at him. How could he not be an alpha if he had literally dicked me into the dirt? It didn't make sense. "How can you not be an alpha?" I pointedly stared at his crotch for a moment, then glared up at him in defiance. I was sure he could remember the knot he'd popped when he'd been railing me. A knot. The thing most people chased, in one way or another, all their lives.

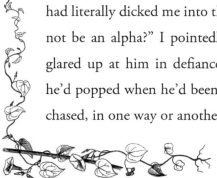

Some of us in different ways than others.

I knew I should've been born with one, whereas Tommy enjoyed his in the rubber variety. Not that I'd ever wanted to know that about my friend, but he was an over-sharer just like I was an under-sharer.

I shook Tommy out of my thoughts, distracted again as Haden's fingers trailed back down to my cheekbone once again. That simple touch shouldn't feel so damn good. Or so fucking sensitive. My toes curled as a shudder tore through my body unbidden.

"A man can only be so many things at once before some start deteriorating, like a village full of buildings where there is only one caretaker. Eventually, no matter what he does, their foundations begin to crumble," Haden murmured in the space between us. His scent was faint but I chased it, my nostrils flaring as a soft throaty chuckle left his lips the moment he noticed what I was doing.

"I don't know if I buy any of that," I grunted. "Seems like a lot of pretty words to explain a shitty thing you did."

"You do not need to 'buy it' for it to be the truth."

Haden's words were fading.

The room was too.

Gray bled around the edges as fog echoed through the corners of my mind.

"It appears as though your time is up, little one," Haden echoed.

"I'm not little." The words were out before I could stop them and then suddenly everything went white.

Sunlight blinded me the moment I opened my eyes, and I was stuck floundering after the puzzle pieces of my dream as I glared up at the stain on our dorm ceiling and tried to calm my heart rate.

When I'd been confused as a kid, I'd decided my thoughts felt like spaghetti. All wiggly and slippery, tangled together in clumps. It had been a long time since I'd felt that way. Since I'd felt the need to summon an imaginary fork and start spooling them all together. Confused, aroused, twist, twist. Till everything was lumped together, even if it wasn't organized.

Somehow it didn't help, though I'm not sure why I was surprised by that.

So instead, I did the only thing I knew how. I sprung into action.

With my backpack slung over my shoulder, still wearing my pajama sweats, I dodged Tommy's muffled "mmm?" from his side of the room and slipped out into the hallway. I'd stumbled home after the graveyard drained, accepting Tommy's apologies, though I knew it wouldn't be the last time he pushed me further than I was ready to go.

The walk across campus was a quiet one at this hour. Most classes didn't start till nine at the earliest on Fridays, so the only place I could really go at...I checked my flip phone...7:45 in the morning was the library on campus.

Yay.

That was sarcasm.

The cool wind whipped my cheeks as I dodged cracks in the sidewalk, superstitious, despite the fact my mother had been dead since I was twelve and as much as I loved my dad, I wasn't sure if I'd regret a crack breaking his back.

The library was surprisingly busy considering the time. Students crammed in corners, their stuffed backpacks like toy chihuahuas sitting loyally at their feet. I wandered my way past them toward the computers at the back of the massive space. They were ancient and yellowed with age, but they always served their purpose. I'd been saving up for a laptop with my measly earnings from the greenhouse I worked at part-time, but it wouldn't be enough for what felt like a hundred years.

My scholarship covered most things. Room, books, and even the omega dorm I lived in currently, not that I wasn't about to change that. What it didn't cover was food. Surprisingly, despite having a lot of "feelings" about me going to college, my dad had, without fail, sent me a monthly allowance for food. I wasn't sure how he came by the money.

Since Mom died, he'd never really been able to hold a job.

He was a lot of things—surly, prideful, confident, and determined. But reliable? Yeah, no.

That was why it was surprising.

Three hours of fruitless Google searches later, I still hadn't found jack shit, even though I'd gotten pretty creative, and momentarily distracted halfway through. I'd corrected myself when I realized the librarians could probably see my search history.

Purple demon dude.

Graveyard demon.

Devil poem.

Hypothermia?

How long does a knot last?

Can you tell how old an alpha is by how long his knot lasts?

65

Knots.

Knots, images.

Dicks, images.

Anatomical dicks, images.

For art.

Not for anything else.

Devil purple guy?

Legends of purple guys in Madison.

Madison legends.

Horny demons.

What is an incubus?

What is the difference between an incubus and a succubus?

Are incubi purple?

Right as I was about to click out of the latest Reddit thread I'd encountered about incubus possession, I felt a prickle at the back of my neck. I wasn't sure if I'd always been naturally aware of others, or if that had been bred out of necessity, but I always, always knew when someone was staring at me.

I whipped around, only to encounter the smiling face of Stinky. Yeah, that's his name. No, I don't know his real name. No, he's not stinky. I guess maybe he used to be or something, but he's not anymore? Or maybe that's my suppressants. Stinky waved at me and slid into the chair beside mine as I casually clicked the little red X at the top of the search page and turned toward him.

"Sup, dude," I nodded, giving the correct dude-bro greeting.

"Sup, dude," he responded politely.

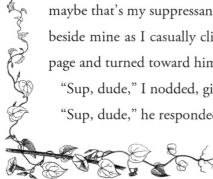

66

I waited. I wasn't sure what I was supposed to say next. Social interactions with people I only kinda knew were always awkward as hell. I wasn't really the most talkative person—and the only person I'd met recently that somehow didn't make the words choke up inside me was Haden, and he was a purple-demon-thing-guy-who-might-or-might-not-be-an-incubus. Even Tommy had been hard to talk to at first, and he was, without a doubt, my favorite person alive.

My frat brothers only knew my surface-level personality, and I was very much okay with that. Even when I attended meetings or parties, they never asked too many questions. Always happy to look the other way so we could fundraise or raise-fun, sometimes both at the same time.

"Excited you're moving into the house, man," Stinky said with a grin. "There's not enough betas. All the alpha stink is enough to make me gag." Again with the whole "alphas stink" thing. *Was my nose broken?* I'd never really thought much about the dirty sock smell, but I guess guys like Tommy and Stinky were less attuned to it.

Maybe they'd grown up with sisters.

"My sisters started gagging when they visited for fall break. Too bad I'll be moving out when you move in."

Ah, that answered that.

"I'm pumped too, dude." I flashed him a grin, which I hoped was the correct response. Apparently, it was because he slapped me on the back five times and ruffled my hair.

I'd be taking Stinky's spot in the house when he moved off campus and I couldn't be more grateful he'd decided to take the leap.

"Can't believe I'm going to have my own place. It's gonna be sick!" Stinky grinned.

"Hell yeah!" I slapped him back five times, as was expected, and his grin multiplied in size before he shoved me away playfully and rose to his feet. Stinky was nice, I decided. I liked him.

Never trust a man named Stinky, Tommy's name popped up in the back of my mind and I flipped him off.

Stinky walked away, and I watched him go till he turned a corner and disappeared behind a line of books, then I opened Google again and started all over.

Dad hadn't ever visited me at college. That didn't mean I didn't see him, though. I'd go home at least once a month to get shoved around by my brothers, whoop their asses at *Mario Kart,* and wait painfully for Dad to let his vitriol out. He was like a kettle sometimes, just bubbling up inside until suddenly the pressure got too much and *whoosh, eeeeee,* the world had to deal with the fury he hid on an everyday basis.

I was the biggest disappointment out of the three of us for obvious reasons, so I always got the majority of his barbed words. Not that Buck and Marvin—*Marv*—ever escaped entirely unscathed, either. We just knew that's how it was. When things were good, they were *real* good, though. Sometimes, Dad would get this look in his eyes, a sparkle, and that night would be filled with laughter, spilled beer, and nachos hot out of the dirty microwave.

I never knew what to expect with him.

Which was why I shouldn't have been surprised when walking home from the library, my phone began to buzz and his name popped up.

The asshole always had to keep me on my toes.

I answered quickly, since I'd already kept him waiting for a ring or two, my heart thumping till my blood ran sluggish. Campus was waking up, sleepy students meandering around, and I dodged their wandering eyes as I ducked off the path so I wouldn't block traffic. The early class-goers were still tucked inside their lecture halls and classrooms, so it was the hungover students that were out and about now, nursing their hangovers in cups, greasy hair crusted to sweaty heads.

It was times like these that I was actually grateful for the scent blockers and suppressants. Meant my nose was blind to their stench.

"I'm coming by next week," Dad's gruff voice echoed from his end of the line, and I shuffled awkwardly, his words not processing. No hello? Nothing? Jesus.

Coming to campus?

To visit me?

His words hit like a sledgehammer and I gritted my teeth, forcing myself to walk through the pain as my breaths came quick and my heart began to stutter. *Why would he come to campus? Why now?* It didn't make sense. He'd never visited me before—

Fuck.

This was why I'd done the whole stupid fucking dare in the first place. Because I'd known at some point, I'd get unlucky enough he'd visit. Not because he cared, no. He wanted to check up and make sure I wasn't spending the money he was sending on shit he didn't approve of. I was the dumb omega. Couldn't be trusted.

"Yeah, sure, Dad." Shit, that wasn't enthusiastic enough. I tried again. "Whatever you want." I wasn't sure what I expected. Once again,

he surprised me as the call ended and I glanced down at my phone in confusion, only to realize that he'd fucking hung up on me.

Whatever.

I shoved my phone in my hoodie and calculated the merits of stopping by a vending machine for a bottle of Mountain Dew before I dove into studying for my next class. It was only when I got halfway home that I fully processed what the hell my dad had said.

A startled laugh burst from my throat and the dude I was passing on the sidewalk gave me a confused look. I just waved him off and continued toward my dorm building, well aware I was muttering like a lunatic.

Shit.

The omega dorm.

I still lived there.

I wasn't going to get to move into the frat until after this semester was over. I was so fucking screwed. Dad was sure to take one look at the building and yeet me all the way to fucking Hell. No way he'd approve. He didn't even want the dean of the college to know I was an omega, not that we'd gotten away with hiding that, and there was no way he'd approve of me living in a dorm full of people that knew his dirty secret.

Walking in and out of the building was like wearing a neon sign that said *omega* on it. That was why I only ever used the front entrance when Tommy was around. Entering through the side always helped with prying eyes, not that I'd ever admit that to him. He already judged me enough for hiding who I was.

I was so fucking fucked it wasn't even funny.

But...

It wasn't entirely hopeless. I mulled over my options as I walked,

hopping up the steps at the back of the dorm building and slipping into the quiet warmth of the indoors that had been my home for over a year. No. It wasn't hopeless. I could lie. I could lie my fucking ass off. Sure, I was shit at it, but I'd have to get real good at it real quick, wouldn't I? And then next time he visited he wouldn't know the fucking difference. Yeah. That's what I'd do. *I'd lie.*

I'd just have to talk to Stinky first.

With my plan in mind, I pushed into our room only to be met with the sharp acrid scent of nail polish remover and Tommy's cheeky grin. He wiggled his toes at me and I rolled my eyes, flopping onto my bed with a quiet huff. I felt unhealthily exhausted, even though I'd really only walked about a mile. Maybe I should've driven the car? But sometimes I liked the cold to clear my head.

With the spaghetti of my Dad's words in my head tangling up with my most recent dream about Haden, I was more than a little exhausted. Tomorrow I'd deal with all of this. Tomorrow. Right now, I just... needed a nap. And a drink.

Damn. I should've bought that soda.

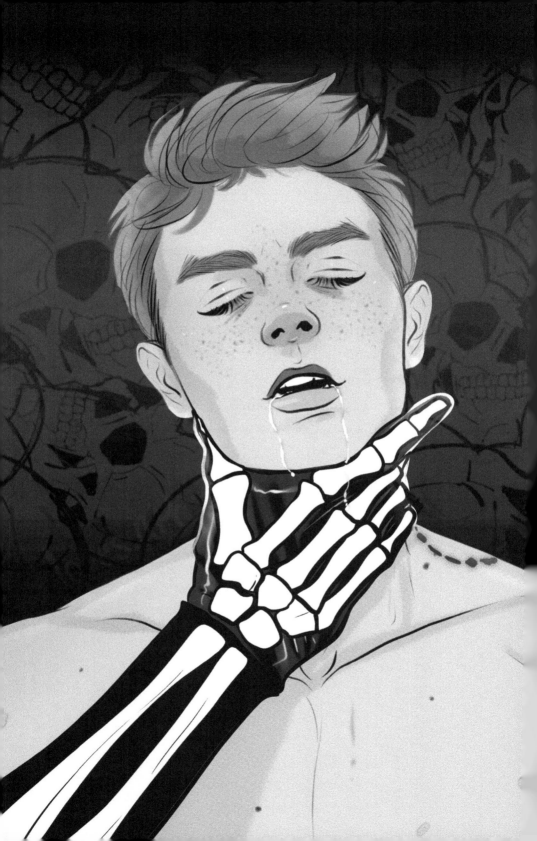

SEVEN

PERCY

The moment the door opened at the frat house, I was met with Frank's friendly but cautious expression. I didn't really know Frank. Not the way I knew Stinky or Brett. Sure, we'd interacted at the events I'd been to, and we shared the customary head-nod now and again, but I was pretty sure I'd never actually spoken to him outside that one amateur football game we'd both played last summer.

The fear of alphas that had been instilled into most omegas by the time they were my age was suspiciously missing due to my upbringing, crushed between the massive sweaty shoulders of my two alpha brothers. So yeah. I didn't know Frank, but he didn't scare me either.

My dad on the other hand…

"Hey man, what's up?" Frank asked, bobbing his head as he leaned in the doorway. He knew I was moving in at the beginning of next semester, and it wasn't like I hadn't been over at least a dozen times as I'd worked my way through initiation. But he was still looking at me like an outsider,

73

and it made my skin prickle.

"Is Stinky home?"

"Nah man, he just went home for the weekend. He's visiting fam." Frank blinked at me. "You chill?"

Was I chill?

Not really.

I was about as far from chill as I could possibly be.

Squirming—on the inside—I shrugged. "Uh, no." I probably should've lied. Said I was "chill" after all. But I could give a rat's ass at the moment what Frank thought of me. If he thought I was a typical "beta basket case," so be it. His eyes widened and he shrugged his massive shoulders, clearly uncomfortable as he tried to shake off my bad mojo. "Is it cool if I go check out his room?"

Maybe Brett would be home.

"To see Brett," I added, covering my tracks.

Frank's eyebrows climbed higher, but he just stepped aside, sweeping his hand toward the front room as I stepped across the threshold. Because I wasn't a fucking heathen, I stomped the mud off my boots, despite the fact there were already muddy footprints all over the shaggy beige carpet.

I headed up the stairs, ignoring the way Frank's gaze made the hair on my arms raise. I could feel his thoughts whirling around me without needing to see his face. *Fucking weirdo.* But I didn't care.

I had a mission.

The hallway was littered with discarded laundry and crumpled red solo cups like it always was. I kicked one aside as I dodged a half-empty laundry basket and swept my way toward the back of the hall where Stinky's room sat. I could hear the soft thrum of music buzzing through the crack in the

door and I sighed, some of the tension bleeding from my shoulders as I knocked on the frame and then pushed my way inside with my shoulder.

"Sup, man." Brett nodded at me from where he was lying, slung across his bed. The rooms here were bigger than the ones me and Tommy had. They were allowed to paint too—which didn't necessarily mean they had taste, or took advantage of the fact. Stinky's side of the room—my side— was painted a deep eggshell blue. I decided I liked it. Just as I had the first time I'd been there when they'd been showing me around that morning after my night in the cemetery when I'd been rubbed raw and fucked open, in more ways than one.

We stared at each other for a moment, the awkwardness palpable in the air as I shuffled in the doorway and Brett sat up straighter. I should probably get used to the weird looks I kept getting. Maybe I looked deranged. Maybe my dad's phone call had fucked me over more than I thought it had? Maybe he could see it on my face.

Maybe I was saying maybe too much, *again.*

I shut the door.

I knew I'd have to give something away if I was going to get what I wanted, though I didn't know what it was. Hopefully not my last bottle of Mountain Dew. I'd learned from a young age nothing was ever free, especially if you wanted it.

"I was wondering if you could help me?" I asked, biting back my pride as the words rattled out like shattered glass. I tried to play it cool, I really did. But I'd never liked asking for help. Ever. I made a point not to, actually, just like I'd made a point to never beg—*unless I was with Haden.* I was stubborn as hell and the last thing I needed was to drop the only shield I had between me and the rest of humanity.

Pride.

I didn't want to ask for help.

But now I needed to.

"So, my dad is coming to town, and he kinda doesn't know where I live," I said quietly because Brett's big brown eyes were all scrunched up like he didn't know what the hell I was smoking. He nodded, clearly waiting for more. When the words got all choked up inside me and the silence grew cloying, he took pity on me.

I tried not to stare at his thick thighs or the fact that he had this cute little dimple on his chin. Tried not to think about much of anything, really. My bond mark throbbed, but I shrugged the pain off as psychosomatic.

"Okay?" Yeah, he threw me a bone, but it wasn't much of one.

"I need to pretend like I moved in here already. That I already live here, I mean." I blinked, the choked up feeling still squashing away inside my throat. Felt like talking around a mouthful of dirt, a feeling I was all too familiar with. This was awkward. Brett knew it. I knew it. God, his shoulders were nice.

My cheeks were hot, and I shuffled awkwardly, suddenly wishing I hadn't decided to wear my usual pair of ratty sweatpants. Should've broken out those jeans Tommy had gotten me for Christmas last year. But they were uncomfortable. And I knew my ass looked amazing in them. Didn't really want to be ogled more than I was at the moment. The attention made me feel naked. Not that dressing up for this would've done me any good.

"Why doesn't your dad know where you live?" Brett asked. And the question should've been an easy enough one to answer. Honestly—most fucking kids didn't have to hide simple shit like this from their parents.

But most kids weren't me, and most dads weren't mine.

He was his own breed.

Pieced together with laughter and hatred, and I was tired of being nothing but a good excuse to let loose that bottled up anger. Being an omega was bad enough, but *disappointing* him too? I couldn't stomach it. Couldn't stomach the consequences either. Honestly, I was more afraid of losing his rationed laughter than I was frightened of his fists.

Bruises healed.

The idea of losing the last part of him I loved, though? God. He was my fucking dad. I couldn't do that. Wouldn't.

So I gave in.

I gave up.

"I'm uh…" The words didn't want to come out. I'd made the decision, but my body wasn't ready as I chewed on my lip and felt Brett's gaze grow heavier, darker. He was annoyed. Starting to be anyway. I couldn't blame him either. *Soldier onward*, I reminded myself. *Don't be a little bitch.* "I'm an omega. He's kinda—" I spoke quicker, ripping the bandaid off, so to speak, then starting over again. "I'm in the omega dorm. And I'm…yeah. I'm not supposed to be."

Actually, what I was saying made no fucking sense. The fact that I was an omega should've meant I was *supposed* to be in the omega dorm. It was my place, beside all the other "breeders". But honestly, I fit in there even less than I fit in here, surrounded by dirty socks and pheromones I was blind to.

"That's fucked up." I wasn't sure what I'd expected to come out of Brett's mouth, but it hadn't been that. I relaxed, the tension bleeding away as a sharp exhale caught in my throat. Okay. So he pitied me at least.

I wasn't above using that against him to get what I wanted, even if that was kinda fucked up of me.

I was fighting a war, though, and even if Brett didn't know it, I was going to win.

I wasn't sure how to respond since he hadn't mentioned what part of that statement was fucked up. The fact that I was an omega trying to move into an alpha house? Or the fact that my dad didn't approve of me living where I was supposed to live. Where I was supposed to be *safe*. Either way, it didn't really matter. So long as I got what I wanted.

Donning my best dude-bro smile I grinned at him. "Right?" I blinked. "So, yeah. I was hoping you could let me pretend I live here next week. Just for like an hour. It won't take long, then I swear I'll be out of your hair.

His face scrunched up as he debated what to do. His t-shirt had ridden up, and I tried not to stare too hard at the happy trail that disappeared inside his jeans. He was bigger than Haden was. But somehow, he didn't light the fire inside me that the purple-demon-thing did. He was just... nice. Pretty. But without substance. Like looking at a McDonald's ad.

Haden was a full-blown buffet.

"Sure dude," Brett grinned back, popping his neck as he leaned forward, his eyes wicked. "But you gotta do something for me in return."

EIGHT

PERCY

I shouldn't have given Brett Tommy's number.

I realized that about twenty minutes later as I was making the drive back across campus, my palms sweaty, and the realization of what I'd just done fresh in my mind. It had been a betrayal, however small, because I knew how Tommy would respond if he knew. And he *would* know. There was no getting around it.

But I'd been desperate.

I tried to wave off the guilt because it wouldn't change what I'd done.

But it festered inside me, this rotting, gnarly thing, curling around my heart as my belly filled with acid.

I shouldn't have given Brett Tommy's number.

I could only pray he wouldn't use it.

But God and I had never had much of a relationship.

Not like the one I had with the Devil, thank god.

I didn't want to go home, so I didn't.

79

So I did what I always did when I started to feel sick of my own shit. I headed to the only place that made me feel whole.

The greenhouse.

I wasn't working today, and the owners always closed on the weekend, but all the employees had been given a key and were encouraged to check on the plants in their free time. I was the only one that ever did it though. It made Mr. and Mrs. Becker way fonder of me than they probably should have been considering the fact I spent half my shifts with a case of soda beneath the front desk, a lollipop in my mouth—or with donuts stuffed into my cheeks like an overgrown chipmunk.

I spent more time at the greenhouse than was probably healthy, actually. Abused the hell out of my access to the building at all hours. But *hell*. The plants made good company, *great* company even. Before the graveyard had become my temporary haunt, this had been my only escape.

I entered the building, more than a little relieved when I confirmed the fact that I was the only one there. The storefront was dark, the break room silent, so I made my way to where the plants were sleeping, my heart lighter already.

My favorite plot was at the back, a rectangle of heaven, surrounded by equipment and foggy plastic. I flopped to the floor beside the baby sprouts and tucked my head in my arms, trying to calm my racing heart.

One of my little buddies had begun to pop out of the dirt, his bright green sprout tipping toward the sky, all hopeful-like. Watching him calmed me the way nothing else did. He was cute. In a baby plant sort of way.

"You're looking good, bud," I told him, chuckling at my own joke a half second after I made it unintentionally. "Bud." I shook my head with

a grin, shuffling closer till I could stare at the lone explorer. He needed water, so I resolved myself to take care of that before I left.

When he was all fully grown, he'd be a glorious yellow squash. I'd eat him. And I'd try not to cry. And hopefully he'd forgive me from squash heaven. Unless he went to squash Hell. But even I wasn't pessimistic enough to believe that would happen.

Realist. See? Fuck you, Tommy.

"I've been a bit of a dick lately." I admitted quietly, because I was pretty sure the squash wouldn't judge. "But I can't really help it." The dirt smelled good. Comforting. Like new beginnings, and I inhaled it greedily as the humid air clung to my skin.

I thought about the grasshopper I buried, absently chewing on my lip as I wondered if he'd ever found his way up to grasshopper heaven. Did grasshoppers and squashes share a heaven? Fuck. Maybe grasshopper heaven was actually squash Hell? Forever cursed to be eaten by little grasshopper hands. I shuddered and shook the thought away because even I knew I was being an idiot.

"I should apologize." I stared at my lil buddy, frowning as I thought about Tommy. About how he'd respond when he found out what *I'd* done. He wouldn't like it, that was for sure. Possibly even the understatement of the century. But maybe he could understand it? Even if he didn't like it.

I hoped anyway.

He was a good friend, even though I felt like a shitty one.

"Ugh, okay. Fine."

After I'd calmed down I bid my plants farewell and rose to my feet, brushing the dirt off my knees with a sigh. This wasn't going to go over well. But hopefully, if I told him before Brett managed to contact him,

then it would mitigate some of the damage. Pulling out my phone, I mulled over the best way to approach this, eventually deciding quick and to the point would be the best. Like ripping off a Band-Aid.

Percy: I gave Brett ur number

Tommy: ?

I could see the chat bubble appear and disappear like a zillion times as Tommy figured out how best to tear me a new asshole. This sucked. It really did. But I'd done it to myself.

Tommy: What the fuck, Percy. You know how I feel about this shit.

Percy: There's more

Percy: I had to tell him I'm an omega

Tommy: Jesus christ. You realize you just sold your soul to the Devil right? He's only going to use this against you. You can't trust alphas, Percy. You know that. They only want one thing, and he'll use you now that he knows.

Tommy: UGH!! 😡 Now I'm going to have to preemptively block him. Send me his number.

Percy: I'm sorry

My cheeks were hot, and my palms were sweaty with regret. I sent over Brett's number, chewing on my thumbnail as I watched the little bubbles appear by Tommy's name again that meant he was typing. Maybe it was selfish of me but I hoped Brett wouldn't decide not to help me when his message didn't go through–if he even sent one at all.

Man. I really was a shitty friend.

My eyes burned.

Tommy: You're a dick.

Tommy: I blocked him.

Tommy: I can't believe you.

Tommy: Stop moping and come home. If you're going to eat your feelings about this at least do it where I know you're safe.

Percy: Are u mad at me?

Tommy: ...

Percy: Sorry

Percy: Dumb question

Tommy: Just come home.

Later that night, as I lay in bed in silence, I mulled over the sting of Tommy's words. He'd been pissed, sure, but instead of railing on me about the number, he'd sprouted a whole rant about dick-o-nauts (his words, not mine) in general.

They only want one thing, he'd said, and I knew he was right.

I *knew* that.

But stubbornly, I wanted to believe he was wrong.

He'll use you now that he knows, Tommy warned me.

I knew that too.

I did.

I just...fuck.

Sometimes just living was so *hard.* Like navigating one of those corn mazes that pop up in the fall where every step you take somehow always ends up the wrong one. Forever stumbling upon dead ends. Maybe I really *was* stupid. But stupidly, I hoped Tommy would forgive me, even if I knew he was never bound to stick around long.

Why would he?

When I was the kind of friend that betrayed him.

I let him use my car though, so maybe I wasn't all bad.

My thoughts were spaghetti again, only they were so twisted up now I had no hope of untangling them. I hoped somehow when I slept I'd be transported again to that foggy place between waking and sleep. The place where Haden lived. Where I wasn't...whatever I was here, and instead, I was a Percy who was made of possibility.

NINE

HADEN

There is nowhere I am safe from Percy's presence. At first, his arrival was easy enough to ignore. The presence of his soul tickled at the back of my mind, like he was searching for the tether between us, though I'd assumed he'd never find it.

I'd been wrong.

In my bed, in the bath, in my office.

He pops up here and there, making small talk with me like his presence isn't an abomination in my personal space. Like the fact he's here at all isn't the most confusing thing that has ever happened to me. He inspires a cautious sort of research to enfold. I need to know how he is doing this. How he is finding me, despite having no magic of his own, aside from a supernatural case of stubbornness.

The feelings he incites frighten me more than his presence does, however.

I had thought I was done feeling.

I suppose I was wrong.

TEN

PERCY

Tommy had yet to forgive me. Sure, he was talking to me, and we still had our weekly movie night. But I could feel this wall between us that hadn't been there before. I wanted to explain to him why I'd done what I'd done, but every time I tried to open my mouth, the words got all stuck inside me.

I didn't know how to tell him that running, lying, fighting—*that* was my life. It wasn't this…test I had to pass. This mission to overcome. It just was. I dodged bullets. That was what I did.

I'd just never had someone I didn't want to hurt before.

I shook away the dark thoughts as my pulse fluttered and I waited with trepidation for Dad's truck to pull up to the student cafeteria parking lot where I'd told him to meet me. The truck rattled. This sound that I recognized before I even saw the withered light-blue paint, or the massive tires. There was this dent in the side from the time I'd driven it when I was seventeen on my way to pick up boxes of Kraft Mac-and-cheese and a six-pack of beer. I'd had twenty dollars in my pocket, an empty belly, and my dad's drunken gaze on my mind, so I'd been more than a little distracted.

I'd paid for that mistake.

Just as I'd paid for every other mistake I'd ever made. Sometimes even the ones I hadn't.

The worst thing I'd ever done to my dad, though, was present as an omega. He'd let me know that, too. That I was the first in his bloodline, that his daddy and his daddy before him had all popped out boys with knots. I was an anomaly. A blip on the family's perfect record.

Realistically, I knew that line of thinking was outdated.

We were in the twenty-first century, for god's sake. Wasn't like you could just pop down to your local market, barter a pig or two, and head home with an omega to fuck. We weren't property anymore and yet somehow, I was still and forever would be lesser in his eyes.

That's why I couldn't let him down.

My pulse throbbed.

My skin was sweaty hot, and I could feel a sick sort of churning in my gut as the truck parked and I watched the door swing open with a creak. Dad stepped out, and I moved to greet him, careful to keep a polite distance, careful not to look him in the eyes. Demure, or some shit.

Sometimes, he liked me like that, all submissive.

Sometimes, it set him off.

I hoped today I'd made the right call.

He grunted a greeting at me and I relaxed. He didn't talk much. Didn't have to. Even with my nose blind like it was, I could normally feel the storm of his emotions brewing on the horizon. Today he was…blank. Which made me nervous. I didn't know what to do to mitigate the

damage if I couldn't tell how he was feeling.

"You gonna show me around this shithole or what, boy?" That was probably the longest sentence he'd say all day and I jumped to attention, stepping onto the pavement, a swing in my step that was more than a little faked.

"This way."

So far everything had gone surprisingly smoothly. Dad hadn't said much when I showed him the class buildings. He didn't mind the cafe, though he was arguably a bit pissed about the prices. I'd had to promise I wasn't squandering away his hard-earned money on froufrou shit (frappuccinos) or overpriced bean-water (black coffee).

We'd even eaten lunch in relative peace.

Dad had paid.

Not that we'd exchanged more than a few grunts as we'd eaten. I asked about Marv's newest omega and he grunted out the words "needy bitch" in response, so there was that. Didn't know if he liked her or not, considering the fact he thought all omegas were bitches. Me included.

Shame curled in my belly as we headed toward Alpha Beta Phi. It was time to show him that I hadn't been lying when I said going away wouldn't mean me falling into more "omega shit."

I knew he wanted to have instilled this deep sense of shame inside of me about it. That he wanted me to hate my designation as much as he did.

But I couldn't.

I was what I was, and there was no changing that, no matter how much

he wished he could.

Being with him reminded me why I did what I did.

Why I hid who I was.

Buried it deep down along with all the other feelings I'd had to swallow over the years.

When we arrived, the house was blissfully empty. The only one home seemed to be Frank, and he'd been steering clear of me ever since our awkward encounter last week. I didn't blame him. I knew how erratic I'd been acting, but that didn't mean I could stop. At least I didn't actually care what he thought of me, or anyone else for that matter.

I was surviving the best way I knew how and that didn't mean making friends.

Or keeping them, my brain unhelpfully added, as guilt eroded at my heart again the second I thought about Tommy and his icy friendliness. Never thought friendliness could feel so impersonal. Like I was a stranger, not the dude he snorted cheetos with at two in the morning.

Dad eyed my cloudy expression, and I stood up straighter, my arms behind my back, feet shoulder-width apart, head down. He relaxed, like me being in a bad mood was, somehow, killing his mood too. Not that I thought he really cared. He cared about me, sure, but in the same way he cared about his truck, or his trailer.

I was his.

His property.

Therefore, what I did reflected on him.

There was no sparkle in his eyes today. No nachos on the horizon. Only stormy weather and the risk of bruises.

The door to the room pushed open and I grimaced as Brett entered. I'd

kinda hoped he wouldn't be here for this. He'd agreed to help me, sure, but it would've been easier to pull off if I didn't have another person lying to worry about. Hell, if he was a bad liar, I was so fucking screwed. Lying through my teeth was hard enough without him here to listen.

"This doesn't look like your shit," Dad finally said, breaking the silence.

He'd been staring at Stinky's side of the room where I'd directed him, and I grimaced, grateful he wasn't looking at me. I'd hoped he wouldn't catch on to that. Though realistically it had been pretty naive of me to think he'd overlook the fact that Stinky's stuff was pretty much all brand new.

"You been spending my money on this?"

"No, Dad." Shit. Shit, shit. I hadn't even thought of that. "Of course not."

"Liar."

My cheeks burned.

I could feel the way Brett was staring at me as he flopped onto his mattress, but I didn't look at him. Neither did Dad, ignoring the other alpha like he was worth little more than dirt. I squirmed. This could go so wrong in so many ways. I wasn't sure why I'd thought this would be a good idea when it was so clearly so, *so* bad.

"My roommate gave stuff to me," I blurted quickly, praying to whatever god was listening that Brett would pick up on my words and play along. Maybe he'd be a good liar? I hoped optimistically.

Dad turned around to look at me and I dropped my eyes quickly, staring at the unshaven bristles on his neck, my pulse thrumming, temples slick with nervous sweat. He had more salt than pepper in his beard now. Not that he'd ever been without it, not as long as I could remember him.

Mom had called him a silver fox.

I wasn't sure what that meant, but when she said it, it'd always seemed like a good thing.

"Look at me when I'm talking to you, boy." My gaze snapped to his face, the feeling of oh-shit-oh-shit only growing louder, my ears beginning to roar. This was different. This wasn't tentatively-happy Dad. This was something else entirely.

Danger, danger, my pulse screamed.

Danger.

Fuck.

Fuck fuck fuck.

Dad's eyes were hazel. They blazed, flickers of orange twisted with vines of poisonous green. Maybe once upon a time I'd thought his eyes were pretty. We shared the same color after all. But now, as I met his gaze, all I saw were the flames of his anger twisting them into something unrecognizable.

Looking at him felt wrong, wrong, *wrong*.

He could sense the danger too, feeding off of it as he huffed out an unhappy noise, our stare down lasting an eternity even though it probably only spanned a few seconds.

"I'm sorry—I didn't mean…" I wasn't even sure what I was apologizing for. For the fact I was lying to him, maybe? For the disappointed curl to his lips? For the way I never seemed to live up to his lofty expectations? Because I'd apparently made him feel like he wasn't good enough, his fragile ego so easily shattered.

"You didn't mean, *what*?" He asked, voice surprisingly soft.

I didn't know what to say because I didn't know what he wanted me to

say. It took me too long to realize he'd been angry because I hadn't looked at him, and my response had been all wrong. Shit. Shit-shit-shit.

Brett was staring at us.

I could feel the weight of his eyes as they bore holes between my shoulder blades. I should be embarrassed, I knew that. Realistically, I should be worried about what Brett thought of me, especially since in a few short months we'd *actually* be living together.

But I couldn't bring myself to care.

I was an ant under a man's shoes, just staring at the foot about to smash me.

"You throw away the shit I bought you?" Dad's voice was deceptively calm.

Danger, danger, danger. My head spun. It didn't matter that he hadn't bought me anything since probably the time I was sixteen and hit puberty. And even then it'd only been a few pairs of shoes over the years as my feet sprouted inches we didn't have the money to pay for.

"No, Dad—" I couldn't help the way my hands began to shake. I squeezed them into fists, the urge to flee buzzing through my body. Flee, always flee. Never fight back. It never did any damn good. Then he'd…fuck. Then he wouldn't smile at me anymore. Fighting back meant losing his forgiveness, and his forgiveness was the only thing that made weathering his storms worth it.

My knuckles turned white, nails biting into my flesh till the sting grounded me. "I wouldn't do that. I swear I still have all my stuff—"

"Then where is it?"

Shit.

Shit. Shit. *Shit.*

92

I couldn't fucking tell him it was sitting peacefully in my real fucking dorm room.

Brett was silent, even the sound of his breathing nonexistent.

I was stumbling upon uncharted territory so I did the thing I did best, I spoke without thinking. "Some of it had holes and stuff so my friend is just…you know. Fixing them?" It seemed like a plausible enough excuse until I saw his face.

Storm clouds. Thunder. Dangerous waters.

"*Fixing* them?" Dad's brow lowered, his jaw flickering with tension. "A few holes and you think shit needs fixed? What the hell is wrong with you?" Clearly he'd been waiting a long time to say this. Or in this case, a few short months since his last rant. "I didn't raise you to be such a goddamn pussy."

I didn't even know what I'd done wrong. Were we really fighting about *holes*? What the actual hell? Even for Dad this was a new low. At least when he'd been angry in the past, it had been because of something normal, like…me being stupid—or crashing his car—or costing him more money because of my suppressants.

Holes?

Why the hell does he care so much about a few fucking holes?

"You think because you got a scholarship at this fancy little shithole you can toss out the stuff I bought you with *my money*?" His eyes flashed. "You too good for your old man now?"

Ah.

And, *finally,* I got it.

Bingo.

This wasn't about my stuff at all, but the fact that he thought I was

looking down on him. Had this whole day been an exercise in tricking me into a corner so he could fight with me about this? Maybe someone at his current job had said shit to him. Something about his son surpassing him or something. Either way, it didn't matter.

It was clear the whole reason he'd come to visit me in the first place was to start something.

I shouldn't be surprised.

I shouldn't.

I knew that.

But my veins filled with ice anyway, and my eyes burned as I stared at my dad's worn work boots and tried not to...to *what*? To cry? *Hell*. The last time I'd cried, I'd been six fucking years old. I didn't get why his anger felt so absolutely shitty now. I'd known he was coming here for something like this, hadn't I? That's why I'd asked Brett for help in the first place.

But deep down, and I could admit this now, I'd been hoping that... fuck. That maybe for once in my life he'd been here because he was proud of me. That he wanted to see what I was making of my life and celebrate it.

I should've known better.

As always, I was just his fucking punching bag.

Annnnd I'd been quiet too long.

Brett's voice made me jump and a warm hand gave my shoulder a squeeze. I flinched back automatically, though I quickly forced myself to relax when I realized it was Brett touching me and not my dad.

Even though I couldn't smell him the way I was supposed to, I still caught a faint whiff of his scent. It was nice, like he was. Bland, though.

Without spark.

"Percy treasures your stuff, sir." Brett dove in without preamble, laying it on thick. All *yessir, no sir, aye aye captain.* My dad ate that shit up like crazy, though. I watched as his shoulders reacted incrementally, his eyes still narrowed and wary. I didn't dare meet them again for fear of setting him off, so I just kept staring at his boots, then his laces, then his boots again.

Brett's hand burned a hole in my shoulder.

It was supposed to feel comforting, but instead, it just felt wrong.

My bond mark itched.

I was glad I'd had the forethought to wear a turtleneck today. I'd made a point to buy a handful more of them with my last paycheck so I could continue wearing them religiously to cover up the back of my neck. Haden's bite had healed but the coloring was stark against my skin, all purple and twisted through with black. Not normal at all. Even if I'd been allowed to mate like the other omegas. All it took was one look at the raised skin to know two things. I was an omega, and something was very wrong with my alpha.

My alpha.

Fuck.

Was that what Haden was?

No, right?

Shit, this was not the time to be thinking about him. My cheeks grew hot, and I zoned back into the conversation only to catch the tail end.

"Real generous of you," Dad said. I wasn't sure what generous thing he was talking about, but I just bobbed my head in response.

"I try, sir." Brett's voice was gentle, but I could still hear the tension.

Dad, thankfully, must not have caught on, though. Hopefully, he couldn't smell the deception in the air along with overripe laundry. I forced my fists to unclench so I wouldn't slice my palms open with my nails.

I don't know how, but I survived the rest of Dad's stay.

As I watched him drive off, his tailgate disappearing around the corner, I forced down the poisonous emotion inside me and, with a grimace, turned toward the back of the parking lot where I'd left my car.

That had gone...exactly as I'd expected.

I'd disappointed him.

He'd been surprisingly cruel.

What hadn't been expected, however, was Brett jumping to my aid. It made me like him a bit more, even if he was an asshole that had forced me to give him my best friend's number.

Speaking of my best friend...*yeah*.

I needed to fix that, too.

No. I *wanted* to fix that. It was different. With Dad, I needed to please him to survive. Tommy, though? Nah. I loved Tommy. It didn't take much thought to realize I'd need to make another effort to make things right.

The idea of heading home to more forced polite conversations was enough to make my head feel like it was about to explode. Enough was enough. I'd bring in the big guns.

ELEVEN

PERCY

"You do know that buying me a bottle of Mountain Dew does not equal an apology?" Tommy said, sounding equal parts amused and exasperated. I turned around, shutting my textbook with a quiet thump. My pulse jumped, my already shitty nerves only growing shittier as I watched Tommy shake the snowflakes from his coat, sling it over our coat rack, and then flop onto his mattress, offending Mountain Dew in hand.

"It was the best thing I could afford," I told him honestly. Though if I was being even more honest, I'd bought it for him because it was my favorite and I thought sacrificing my last soda to him would make him realize how sincere my apology was.

He narrowed his eyes at me. His hair was all done up like it was when he went out clubbing. Tommy liked to pull, though he never brought his conquests home. I wondered if it was because he thought I'd find it weird he only ever fucked other omegas. But I didn't.

"Did you buy yourself one?" he asked, his manicured eyebrow still

97

arched. My cheeks flushed, and I shook my head. Hadn't had the money. After spending my extra cash on filling up my car and new turtlenecks last week, I'd been running short. Working part-time didn't cover much of anything after I paid for my textbooks.

Tommy's eyes narrowed, and he pursed his lips, *hmm-ing* and *haa-ing* for a moment before ultimately making his decision. I must've looked real pitiful because he patted his mattress like he was beckoning a dog, and I immediately launched myself at him.

"Well, that changes things!" He pulled me into a headlock, ruffling my hair with a manicured hand before he shoved me to the other side of the bed and sighed.

"I couldn't buy another one." I blinked at him, going for pitiful. Apparently he liked pitiful because he just laughed, rolling his eyes heavenward.

"God, your puppy eyes," Tommy huffed.

I batted my lashes.

He shoved at my chest.

I batted my lashes again.

"Okay, okay." Tommy grinned at me, the ice melting between us. "I forgive you." He held up a finger sternly, "But only if you really truly regret your actions and you promise to never do it again."

For most people, a phone number wouldn't be such an issue.

But I knew Tommy.

And I knew I'd broken his trust. For him, it wasn't about the *what* of it, but the *why* of it.

"I missed you," I said, because sometimes saying I'm sorry was really fucking hard.

"I missed you too, you big jerk," he huffed with a wry grin, shaking his head. "It's not like I was ignoring you."

"Yeah, but you weren't being...*you,* you know?" It had been lonely. My heart throbbed.

"Ah." Tommy's grin faltered, and he sighed, pinching the bridge of his nose before dropping his hand and leaning over to give my thigh a gentle squeeze. "Trust you to give me those fuck me eyes and not even know it. But yes. You're right. I was putting some distance between us."

I grimaced. *Fuck me eyes?* Yeah, fucking right.

Tommy was the second person to say that, though Haden hadn't been quite so crass.

Whiiiich just reminded me of Haden again.

"Any luck tracking down your mystery alpha?" Tommy asked curiously. He'd gone from murderous to murderously curious. Which was a vast improvement.

I sighed and shrugged. "Haven't been looking."

"Then why do you look all fucked up today?"

I looked fucked up? I peeked over at the mirror on the closet door that Tommy had installed and grimaced when I realized he was right. Dark circles. My tawny brown hair sticking up in sweaty spikes. Chapped lips. Pale. Ugh. I really did look fucked up. "Dad came to visit."

"No shit?"

I hadn't told him when Dad was coming. After the whole blow up thing and the "alphas are shit" conversation, I hadn't been ready to hear another rant about how shitty my dad was. I already knew that. Hearing about it didn't change reality, just made me feel powerless and a little pathetic.

I loved Dad.

I couldn't stop, even though I knew I shouldn't. Even though I knew it was bad for me. Even though I knew that there should be a limit to love, that it shouldn't be bottomless. When someone makes you feel like a fraction of yourself, the love should stop. But it didn't. It never had. I loved him anyway. Even when he hurt me, sometimes especially then. I could see how twisted he'd gotten inside, and I'd always hoped that one day he'd get himself untangled.

Even now, the fact that I was disappointing him—hurting him—only made me feel worse than his anger.

Because I knew deep down, beneath all that bite, he was just a scared old man who'd lost too much too soon and something had broken inside him that could never be fixed. No matter how much I loved him. No matter how much I forgave him.

Tommy got the tequila out again.

Somehow, he got me talking too. My words were stilted. Awkward. But the longer I talked, the easier it became until suddenly, talking didn't make me feel like I was choking up shards of glass anymore. He stroked my back in that friendly way he always did, booted up a movie on his laptop, and when the lights flickered off and the screen flashed to the main menu, he gently nudged me with the Mountain Dew bottle I'd given him.

"I don't even like this stuff," he said quietly, poking me in the ribs. "But I know you do." My cheeks burned and my eyes began to sting. I took the bottle, fumbling with it as I cradled it protectively to my chest. "The fact you gave it to me means a lot, so thank you," Tommy added sincerely.

"You're welcome." The words came out choked, and I curled around my knees, making myself as small as I could as I stared at the laptop screen and thanked the gods I hadn't lost the only friend I'd ever had.

TWELVE

HADEN

When I woke, the boy was back. Percy. It had been a few days between his last visit and now. Not that I was keeping track, because I most assuredly was not (seven days and three hours since his last visit.) But he was back. I still wasn't sure how he was here at all. It seemed I'd have no choice but to find a new source for the research I was conducting to discover the truth of his peculiar housecalls. So far, he didn't seem to comprehend that this place was real, that while he was here, he affected things just as he did when he was in the land of the living.

I should send him away.

Banish him.

Cut his soul tether from mine and be done with it all.

But…

As he lay sleeping inside my bed—this was a first; normally, he was awake when he visited—I had no choice but to admire him.

Percy's hair was tragic. It was matted to his head, his skin sallow, the dark circles under his eyes blossoming with bruises. His soft pink lips were raw and gently parted, full cheeks cleanly shaven despite the hour. His hands were tucked underneath his face, his naked body curled up tight, like he was trying to take up as little space as possible despite the width of his broad shoulders.

As I'd noticed the last few times I'd seen him, the freckles that were scattered across his cheeks stopped there. Instead, there were moles that danced across his porcelain skin—his arms, his shoulders, his collarbone. I traveled between them, tracing the valleys and dips of his surprisingly muscular body with my eyes, a curiosity I hadn't felt in eons thrumming under my skin.

The smattering of hair on his chest was sparse. His sweet nipples full and flushed where they sat atop the shapely swell of his pectorals. I wanted to sink my teeth into the meat to feel the give of it. The desire to touch was so visceral it nearly took my breath away.

I spared a single glance for his thick hips, his long muscular legs. Forcing myself not to ogle just because I had never had another man in my bed. *Anyone* in my bed, actually.

Which posed the question…

"Why are you in my bed?"

Percy startled awake. His thick brown lashes fluttered as his eyes shot open and he stared at me, seemingly more shocked than I was to discover that he was in bed with me, despite being the one that had traveled here in the first place.

"Sorry." Percy's apology was half-hearted at most. I forced back a smile, conflicting emotions buzzing inside me as I realized, belatedly, that once again, he must've been searching for me. This time while he wasn't

consciously doing so. Part of me wanted to gloat.

The other part of me, the bigger part, the sensible one stamped down on those feelings, crushing them to ruin.

"You're back," I commented, waiting for his reply. He had the strangest way of talking. Informal. Crude. Honest. It was refreshing when all day I spent with textbooks and obligations, commanding respect from my inferiors as there was no way to rule without it.

"I guess I am." Percy continued to stare at me, and I wasn't sure what to make of his expression.

It had been a long time since I had needed to decipher someone else's moods like this. Maybe never. No matter. I shook the feeling away, forcing down the flicker of life that ignited inside me as his hazel eyes grew wide and soft.

They were littered with spots of orange, like sparks, though the overall mossy green reminded me of springs I had long since forgotten, whether that was by choice or because of time, I could no longer remember either. However, the longer I watched him, the darker his eyes became, his pupils flooding his irises as I watched his lips part once more.

Tapping into instincts from my past, I searched for the sound of his heartbeat.

It was faint.

Thud, thud, thud.

Rabbit-like and rapid.

My response to the sound surprised me more than Percy showing up in my bed did. My cock thickened, throbbing as my gums began to ache with the need to bite. My skin grew hot, my chest fluttering. There was this urge inside me I couldn't seem to fully sate—to grab him. To force him to his belly. To taste his submission on my tongue. To mount him till he howled my name, and his sweet hole clutched velvety-hot around my cock.

He'd been so tight that night in the cemetery. Slick. Squeezing around me till my head spun and the urge to fuck became impossible to deny.

I flinched, shoving away the feelings, hiding behind apathy as my heart began to race with fear. *What in Thanatos's name was going on?*

"What brings you here?" I asked, forcing myself to speak, to act normal. This should not be difficult. He was nothing. A mistake I'd made over a month ago. That was it. Albeit a very delicious mistake, but—no. No. I needed to stop thinking that way. "You must've wanted something if you're back so soon."

I couldn't have him a second time.

I *shouldn't* have him a second time.

Already I could feel my resolve weakening.

Gods help me.

"I want to forget," Percy's voice wobbled. Concern ebbed inside me, yet another emotion I'd left behind. What did he want to forget? Me? If that was the case, he should really stop coming here. It was hard to move on when I could practically taste him in the air.

Staring at me would do him no favors.

"You want to forget that night in the graveyard?" I clarified.

Then he surprised me, shaking his head no. His hair looked light, downy soft though it was slicked with perspiration. I wanted to comb it away from his forehead, stroke away the tension between his brows, though that feeling wasn't one I was ready to confront.

How was it possible he did not regret the graveyard?

I did.

I had thought of it every day since it happened. It had been a mistake, surely he thought so too? Our last encounter had given me that impression, anyway. But…maybe I'd misread him.

It was possible.

Those impossibly sad eyes blinked up at me, and I desperately tried not to search for his faint scent in the air or the throb of his nervous pulse. Though the instinct had been dead for years, I had unfortunately already woken it. All it took was a thought for the steady *thump, thump* of his racing heart to fill my head with cotton.

I swallowed, waiting for him to continue.

"No." Percy's voice was a honeyed whisper. "I don't regret that night." Though he clearly regretted *something*. "I regret every night since."

I stared at him.

Thump, thump, thump.

My dick pulsed and the feeling was so foreign it made my head spin. It would be so easy to grab him like this. To push his thighs open and force my cock inside him. He'd like it too. I could see the way he was watching me, pupils blown black with lust, his tongue flickering out to wet his lips.

"My life is a nightmare right now and I can't seem to wake up from it," Percy admitted quietly. He looked so…sad. His expression forlorn. Reminded me too much of Cerberus when he begged for scraps. I didn't know what to do with that face. Didn't know what to do with him at all.

His heartbeat quickened.

I chased the sound of it, my fingers clenching into fists. I shouldn't humor him. I shouldn't be listening to him at all.

"Your life is a nightmare and your response is to seek me?" It didn't make sense. He should be scared of me. It was clear I wasn't human

anymore. I didn't even remember what it was like to be one.

"I guess." Percy shrugged, clearly unable to disagree.

Again, I was floored.

I didn't know what to say, my skin too tight, my head fuzzy as I forced myself to hold very still for fear of frightening him. It was not lost on me, the irony that he'd only been in my bed for minutes and I'd gone from wanting him out of it, to wanting inside of him.

What was it about him that made my skin itch?

"Are you looking for distraction, pup?" I asked, because I wasn't sure why else he'd be here, why else he'd find me of all people. I couldn't give him what the living could. In fact, the longer he stayed here, the more dangerous it became for the both of us. Living souls were not meant to remain in my kingdom for long, or at all. Not that it had stopped Percy thus far. Regardless of how he managed to get here, his soul could not stay too long lest he risk it losing its way back to his body.

"I'm looking for escape," Percy corrected me. Cheeky. Sad. A juxtaposition that made me endlessly intrigued. How could one have so many emotions at once? So many that I couldn't keep track of them as he shuffled on my silken sheets, his lovely nose scrunched up in frustration, his eyes shining with desperation.

Desperate for me to save him.

From what?

Himself?

I could not be an escape and he should not seek me like this. Devil, demon, King—I had been called all these things. My purpose was to hand out punishment, torture, and justice. I had spilled more blood than tears, severed hope, created balance. I could be relied upon for many

things. I could be called many things. But…never once had I been called "comforter." Never once had a man lay naked in my bed, his eyes lost, praying to me for absolution from sins he had not committed.

Touch me, his eyes pleaded.

Help me forget.

"I don't think I can give you what you want." He wanted *gentle.* He wanted an emotional connection. Something I wasn't capable of. I wasn't sure if I ever had been. That was why I'd been chosen for this job, after all.

"Please?" The word was nothing but a breath. So quiet if we hadn't been mere inches apart, I might not have heard it. It was a simple word. One I heard often. But not like…this. Not from him. He'd been so reluctant to beg me before that now…hearing that word from his lips so readily…fuck.

My dick throbbed, and I had to force myself not to touch, so surprised by the intensity of my own desire, I didn't know what to do with myself.

Please, he said.

So sweetly.

Like it cost him nothing to give this to me.

And then I felt the gentle brush of his fingertips as they stroked over my cheek and my resolve continued to crumble.

"You gave it to me once before," Percy reminded me, words soft. Memories of what exactly I'd given him assaulted my senses. I fought back a groan, my own lashes growing heavy as my balls began to ache. I had given him something that night. Something I hadn't even known I could give. I'd fucked him in every definition of the word. Plowed into his slick hole till his pleasure dripped down my sac, till he'd sobbed, till his fat pink cock had leaked all over the dirt.

"You called so sweetly for me then." The words left my lips without permission. I shouldn't be reminiscing like this. Or at all.

"I'm calling you now."

And so he was.

"Are you?" I teased, surprised that I was capable of flirting back.

Percy pursed his lips, and then the most wonderful thing happened. They twisted up, his face scrunching as he fought back a smile that eventually pushed through. It was a nice smile. Like summers long forgotten. Boyish. Sweet. Awkward, like the expression was as foreign to him as it was to me.

When I could do nothing but stare he rolled his eyes, expression playful as his questing fingers paused their movement, and he lay his palm flat along my cheek.

It was so very warm.

He smelled like blossoms and citrus. *Sweet.*

"Alpha…" Oh Gods. My lashes fluttered and I fought back a groan as his plaintive croon echoed like a promise between us. His low, scratchy voice should not affect me so, I knew this. The word was stilted, awkward. Like he didn't know how to use it, like he'd never done it before. The fact I was his first—even if I knew I wasn't what he thought I was—made my fangs itch and my dick flex.

I cocked my eyebrow, not that he could see it behind my mask. I was glad for that last barrier between us.

"I need…" Percy continued, just as unsure, just as stilted as before. Perfect. Absolutely perfect. Endearing as all hell.

"You need…?" I waited.

Percy's freckles scrunched up again. I wanted to bite the tip of his nose.

Fingers fidgeted along my skin as he debated with himself. He was trying to seduce me. I didn't have the heart to tell him he couldn't do that. I didn't function like men did. Emotions were far from reach, especially those regarding affection or sex. Not that it was proving to be true anymore, however.

Clearly, Percy had magic of his own.

Having already made up his mind his eyes narrowed and his jaw ticked with determination. Then, with stilted, shy movements, his fingers quested down to my chest. He lay his hand there, right over where my heart should beat. Maybe he was searching for it, or maybe, like I suspected, he just didn't know what to do next.

His innocent, awkward seduction had me tied in knots around his little finger.

Against all odds, his fumbling inexperience made the beast inside me threaten to break free.

"Help me forget?" How we'd gone from *I want to* forget, to *help me* forget made my head spin. Percy's fingers slipped lower. He traced over the fabric of my shirt, tucking into my belt loops with a gentle tug. He was so close to my dick I couldn't help the way my hips pushed toward his questing fingers. Percy looked conflicted, his brow twisted up, his mouth made of soft pink lines. Like he knew what he wanted but he had no idea how to get it.

Like I was standing in the way between him and my cock.

Fuck.

"You're forgetting your manners, omega." I reminded him, because one does not openly reach for another's cock. But he just shrugged sheepishly, his pink tongue flickering out to wet his lower lip.

"Please?" He tried again, brow still furrowed, eyes blazing. So awkward. So earnest.

I groaned, unable to help myself. Like a dog with a bone he'd latched onto my weakness. Fire flickered in his eyes and his lips twisted up into a pleased grin that made me realize I was dealing with a bigger brat than I'd anticipated.

"*Please*, alpha?" Good Gods. The fumbled phrase made my belly flip.

"I shouldn't." I stared at his naughty little mouth, unable to help myself as desire thrummed beneath my skin. I wanted to close the distance between us and bite those already bitten lips, then soothe the sting with my tongue. It seemed unfair how far away he was at that moment, even though it was merely inches.

At war with myself, I stared at him.

Maybe my feelings were a fluke.

Maybe I wasn't supposed to feel them at all, but in that moment I couldn't stop the long-dead instincts that threatened to take hold of me again.

"The first time was already too much for the both of us, clearly," I added, though I already knew I was seconds from giving in.

My gaze caught on his neck. Peeking between the meat of his shoulder and its gentle slope was my bite mark. I traced over the shape of it with my thumb, surprised by how quickly it had healed, given how deeply I'd bitten. I hadn't meant to be so rough, but then—like now—he brought something out of me that I had never known existed.

"I'll be good," Percy swore, like that had ever been an issue to begin with.

That simple promise, against all odds, broke the last of my resolve.

"Of that I have no doubt." I squeezed the back of his neck, my thumb

pressing hard against the bite mark as his eyes rolled back. His sweet little tongue curled inside his mouth between his parted lips as endorphins lit up his system from the pressure. Somehow I knew this, as I pressed down harder and watched him grow limp with pleasure. "You are eager to please, in a way most never are."

Somehow he still managed to speak, despite the fact I was actively collaring him. "I'll do whatever you want."

Apparently something even as intimate as this wasn't enough for him. Stubborn.

Still, harder I pressed, forcing myself not to groan as his lashes fluttered and his eyes rolled back a second time. "You give yourself away too freely."

Percy bit his lip, his pearly white teeth catching at the pink flesh. They were little. *Cute.* Cute like he was. Slightly crooked, in an endearing way, his canines bigger than most omegas, just like the rest of him.

His lashes still fluttering, he reached for my other hand and I let him take it, intrigued by what he had planned. He'd been so full of surprises I wasn't sure what to expect. When he brought my fingers to his lips, I had only a moment to mentally prepare before the slick wet-hot of his tongue was lapping at them.

Flick, flick, suck.

Ugh.

My eyes grew heavy with lust, my cock throbbing in time with the tentative, unpracticed swipe of his tongue. Before, when he'd done this, I'd been wearing my gloves so as much as I'd enjoyed the visual stimulation, I hadn't gotten to feel the heat of his mouth like this. This time he'd caught me in the middle of a break in the work day. In a fit of frustration, I'd tossed my gloves aside, toed off my boots, and lay on my bed, waiting for my energy to return.

Lately, I'd lacked the drive to do things I'd always done.

I didn't want to blame Percy, but privately, I acknowledged the fact that he was always on my mind. It was clearly affecting me.

I *shouldn't* give in to him. But I'd already played this game of hot and cold with myself and obviously, my desire for him had won the moment he curled his tongue around my middle finger, sucking me far enough down I could practically feel the back of his throat. All tight and wet. Seemed obvious that it should be wet, but I had never really thought about it before. Not before I'd met him, anyway.

I groaned as Percy swallowed, his teeth gently scraping my fingers as he pulled off, only to sink down once again. It was easy enough to picture another part of my body in his mouth, but somehow this felt filthier. His eyes were hooded, this determined twist to his brow that practically screamed how desperate he was to please me.

And then he sucked me too far down and choked with an unhappy cough, pulling off, his eyes watering, lashes wet.

My pulse throbbed, and my dick jerked at the sight. Watching him struggle was its own kind of pleasure. The way his face turned splotchy red, the way his lips stretched wide, and tears leaked down his cheeks. How *frustrated* he looked. Angry that he'd been unable to accomplish what he'd set out to do.

He was glaring at me, as if daring me to tell him that he'd failed.

To tell him that he wasn't good enough.

"If you keep looking at me like that, there will be no saving you," I warned, that *something* deep inside me that had begun to wake, clawing toward the surface. Tooth and nail tore through my carefully constructed walls, howling to get out.

"I don't want to be saved," Percy huffed, with his face scrunched up in annoyance. The expression had me half amused, half panting to shove my cock in his mouth and watch him choke again.

"You do," I whispered, letting go of my inhibitions as I traced his lower lip thoughtfully, even though what I really wanted to do was shove my fingers back inside his mouth. I pulled his bottom lip down, admiring the pretty pink of his gums and his pearly little teeth before I let it *thwap* back into place. He glared at me and I couldn't help my reaction. The moment he made that frustrated face again, I was pressing my finger back inside, rubbing along his tongue till it curled and he began to suck obediently.

The urge to make him choke was hard to shove down, but I managed.

He was so fucking sweet it made my teeth hurt.

"You want to be saved," I murmured, unable to recognize my own voice, it had grown so rough. "Though why you've chosen my cock as your savior, I cannot understand." Percy scoffed around my finger, though the noise was muffled, his eyes bright with indignation and desire.

I had no choice.

I broke.

I shoved him down, climbing over his body in one swift movement. He opened for me, his thick thighs spongy with sweat, the muscle dense when I grabbed his inner thigh and shoved him wider. Inside his mouth, I forced my finger deeper, before slipping in a second digit to watch him struggle, eyes watering, his hard cock knocking against my lower abs.

He didn't fight, succumbing to the pleasure torture with surprising grace.

He was beautiful this way.

He gave in so eagerly, unpracticed, but enthusiastic. His eyes were nearly black with lust as his lips stretched around my fingers and I began to play with him. Out, in. Toying with the slick heat of his tongue till I watched the tension bleed from his shoulders and his brow knit with concentration.

Percy wanted to please me.

I could not fathom why.

Why would he give in to a creature like me? Why give himself away? It made no sense. *He* made no sense. A walking contradiction. His large body so gloriously submissive, his frustration flavored like desperation. He was confusing and contradicting, and entirely fucking perfect.

I should not like this as much as I did. Maybe something was wrong with me. Gods were not meant to bow to mortals' whims. But watching him focus on pleasing me, watching the way his mind quieted, pleasure fogging his expression, was enough to make me give up on all my hang ups so that I could watch him fly.

"You are thinking too much," I whispered. Despite the fact he was more relaxed than when he'd arrived, I could still sense his tension. He wanted to let go. I could see it on his face, but there was something blocking that release.

Percy whimpered, a pitiful little sound.

I slipped my fingers free, forcing myself not to reach down and give my cock a sympathetic squeeze. He looked overwhelmed.

Maybe…he needed *more?*

Or maybe…he needed *less?*

Yes.

Less.

"You are too sensitive," I decided. "Overstimulated." Yes. I was sure of this now.

Percy stared at me, clearly confused. Though he made an unhappy noise as I pulled away from him, his fingers dragging my shirt as he tried to pull me back down.

"Lie still, pet." I urged, trying to hold back my laughter. He looked so annoyed it was almost comical. I'd hardly moved. But, to soothe him, I didn't leave the bed. Instead, I reached for the nightstand, fumbling around till I found what I wanted.

Percy eyed me distrustfully as I returned, my precious cargo held between us. The black silk slipped between my fingers and I arched a brow, waiting for him to give up.

"Why do you have that?" Percy asked, lovely eyes narrowed. He looked wary. Nervous. My dick twitched and I bit back a groan. *Why did he affect me so?* It wasn't natural.

"Open your legs, dearest." I didn't answer his question. He didn't need to know that information. He let me back in between his legs with a petulant huff to hide the very real need in his eyes, and I settled into my rightful place, cock bumping against all that lovely, speckled skin. I didn't mind the scars, I had plenty of my own.

"I don't know if I…" Percy trailed off, biting his lip as I leaned over him.

"If you do not like it you can always say no," I promised, waiting for his response.

"But what if I don't…" Percy trailed off a second time, chewing on his lip. I wasn't sure what about being blindfolded made him so nervous, but it was up to him whether or not he was ready to take what I was willing to give him.

Now that I'd given in to my own desires, there was no use doing things halfway.

I watched a war wage across Percy's face. His nose scrunched up, his brow furrowed, lovely hazel eyes dark with need and fear. He bit his lip, further abusing the already torn flesh. Then, like magic, the battle ended. Sunlight broke across his stormy features and Percy relaxed, having chased off whatever demons were haunting him as he gave me a nervous little nod.

"I will care for you," I promised, voice a quiet rumble. Percy was visibly shaking, his rounded shoulders drawn tight, his eyes haunted and hunted, both. "*I will care for you*," I repeated, more seriously, using one hand to gently stroke over the swell of his cheekbone. His lashes fluttered.

And then he nodded again, this time more sure. Confident.

I tied the blindfold carefully around the back of his head, stroking over his sweat-sticky curls, tracing the shell of his pink ears. He was sensitive there because he shuddered, then twitched as I leaned back to admire my work.

Without all of his senses, I hoped he would be able to relax. That the sensation of my touch would be heightened. That the demons he fought would remain hidden out of sight.

Sweet rabbit.

So tired from running he ran right into the arms of a wolf.

"Can you see?" My voice was nothing but a murmur. Still, he heard it.

Percy shook his head. He looked lovely like that. Swathes of flushed tan muscle spread out beneath me, filling up my bed with his sunshine and sweat. I wanted to taste the salty skin at the base of his throat, nuzzle into the damp skin at his groin and inhale his musk till I had the flavor

memorized. "Good."

I stroked along his cheeks, keeping my touch innocent at first as I traced between his freckles like they were constellations in the sky. I missed stars. Somehow I'd forgotten that. His skin was covered in downy soft peach fuzz, not a lick of facial hair in sight. I wondered if that was because he was an omega, or if it was something inherently Percy.

There were many things about being human I'd lost over the years. Maybe I'd need to brush up on them if I was going to keep him.

No.

No.

Not keep.

I shouldn't.

I couldn't.

Right?

But he *did* look perfect spread across my dark sheets. A beacon of light in a world made of shadow. I traced over the swell of his lower lip, unable to help the arousal that bubbled up inside me as they parted and a soft little puff of hot air met my skin.

"Focus on my touch. Pay attention to how it feels," I murmured, watching his pulse flutter. *Thump, thump, thump* went his heart. "Think about what I may do next. Anticipate it, *relish it.*"

He inhaled shakily as I traced back over to his ears, stroking along the velveteen skin so I could watch him squirm again. It took him a while. But the longer I played, the more relaxed he became. Several minutes later, after I'd memorized the features of his face with my touch, Percy finally went lax beneath me.

Beautiful.

I couldn't help myself, my hand slipping lower, fingers wrapping around the long column of his throat possessively. He didn't tense up again. His heart beat stuttered against my palm.

How could all this be mine?

If not forever, then in that moment.

He was far too lovely to be here. Far too lovely to be sullied by my touch. And yet, he caved for me, let me hold dominion over him in a way no one should be allowed to. I squeezed his neck tighter, power thrumming through my body, arousal white hot in my veins. *How far would he let me go?* He didn't move, didn't so much as flinch from the pressure, though his pulse continued to thump erratically, and his body began to grow stiff once again.

"I can tell this is difficult for you," I encouraged him softly. He shook. "But you submit so beautifully, pup." The most beautiful thing I'd ever seen. In a way, he reminded me of the puppies I raised down in the pits. The way they'd fight each other for scraps of attention, always earnest, if not naive.

It was clear from the way his lips thinned that he disagreed with the compliment. It wasn't like I often handed them out, but even still, the words to soothe him quickly rose to the tip of my tongue.

"If I say that you are beautiful, then you are." His pulse thrummed beneath my palm, his airway carefully pinched, but not hard enough that he would no longer be able to breathe. I refused to harm him. "I do not lie."

"But, maybe you're biased." The cheek on him.

"Why?" I thumbed over his collarbone, drinking in the startled little gasp he made. "Because I bit you?"

He didn't make sense.

How he could think I would bite him without finding him beautiful was itself a contradiction. As much as I'd lost the human part of me, even I knew what he proposed was preposterous. That I would sink into his heat only because of carnal delight? No. There was something else there. A beauty flickering through the tension in his muscular form. It made me drunk, like every twitch of his supple thighs, or tremble of his pectorals was like taking a sip of wine, making me drunk on desire.

Percy began to shake again, and I loosened my grip on his neck, simply holding it now as I let him gather himself together. His nipples were hard, and I fought back the urge to lean down and lick them, instead swiping my thumb across one of their pebbled peaks with my free hand. Percy jolted, a little whimper escaping his lips. My cock ached in response.

"You bit me and ran," he accused, his voice wobbling with pleasure and vitriol.

"I do not run," I scoffed.

"Fine." The muscle in his jaw flickered with tension. "You *left* then."

I suppose I couldn't argue that.

"Would you rather I stayed?" I flicked his nipple to emphasize my point. Gently. But he still jumped like his entire body was electrified by the fleeting touch.

Percy gritted his teeth and I could feel the way his cock was leaving a sticky patch on the front of my shirt. I wanted to inhale the sweet musk of his arousal, though I was admittedly confused why his scent was so faint. Maybe it had something to do with suppressants he'd mentioned. A side effect. I didn't know what exactly they were, but it didn't take a genius to guess from his words that they weren't taken for pleasure.

Percy mulled over my words, the tension in his body obvious. Basking in the beauty of his torment, I moved to the other side of his chest, playing with him till every brush of my fingers had him pushing into the touch.

It took a long time for his answer, but when he did, it came in the form of a plaintive whine.

"*That* is not a yes or no answer, pup."

Percy gritted his teeth again, clearly annoyed. I liked annoying him. It made him do things like push up against me, his heat brushing against my own, like he was now. I wished then that I was as bare as he was. That I could feel the way our sweat-slick skin stuck together, our heavy cocks pulsing with desire as they ground against one another. A communion of sin and pleasure I had never thought I'd want to indulge in.

"I don't know." Percy squirmed.

To reward his honesty, I pressed more insistently between his thighs, the weight of my hips dragging my cock against his to remind him what we both wanted. "If you do not know, then I suppose I made the right choice, don't you think?"

"By leaving me?"

"By leaving you with a *choice*." I was growing tired of this conversation. I wanted Percy's whines back, even though I'd been the one to force him to speak in the first place. He was fascinating either way, but that didn't mean I was thinking with my head at the moment.

"Oh…" Percy trailed off, his voice thick with emotion as I gave his hips a squeeze before stroking over the thickness of them. I dug my thumbs into his hip bones just to feel the give of his flesh before the hard bone bit back.

He tensed up again like he'd only just realized he'd been naked all

along. I couldn't stop my grin. He squirmed again, and watching him wriggle made my balls draw up tight and my gums ache to sink my fangs into all that gloriously tanned skin.

Percy's cock was hard.

So hard.

I wanted to touch, but I wanted him to beg for it again even more.

"You are the one crawling into my bed," I whispered, watching the way he grimaced because he knew it was true. His skin was flushed, the pink spreading down the column of his throat. His Adam's apple bobbed against my palm as he swallowed. My grin turned meaner, not that he could see it. I hardly recognized the feeling on my own face. "You are the one who craves my cock so badly that you beg for it."

Percy shuddered, and the way his abs tensed made my head spin.

"If you allow me to own you, there will be no more choices. When you are mine, I will not let you go." I knew this to be true even if I'd never so much as thought those words before. To own someone else—meant belonging to them in turn. I wasn't sure that was a promise I could make. Wasn't sure it was a promise I *wanted* to make. But, I did want to make my point, so I didn't mince words.

I leaned down, my tongue laving over one of the still taut nipples on Percy's chest. When I tasted him, he groaned, low and deep, his pelvis bucking up against mine. *Sweet puppy.* His hips jerked upward again, searching for friction, and the moment he found it he couldn't seem to stop, humping the ridge of my cock with little care for how desperate it made him appear.

I loved it.

"I do not share," I warned him. "I am stubborn. I am possessive." I bit his other nipple to emphasize my point. As much as I wasn't sure I wanted to keep him at all, he needed to realize that this wasn't a fantasy. I was a god, but I was not perfect. Though…I also didn't want to frighten him off, so I soothed my bite with another eager suck and listened to the way his breath grew stuttery-soft and the tendons in his neck tensed. "I am all those things…but I am also fair." Another kiss. "Though, be warned. Gods do not share their play things."

When he came I made him lick up the mess he'd made on my sheets, and mere moments later, before I had a chance to say goodbye, he disappeared.

Just like that.

His light absent like it had never been there at all.

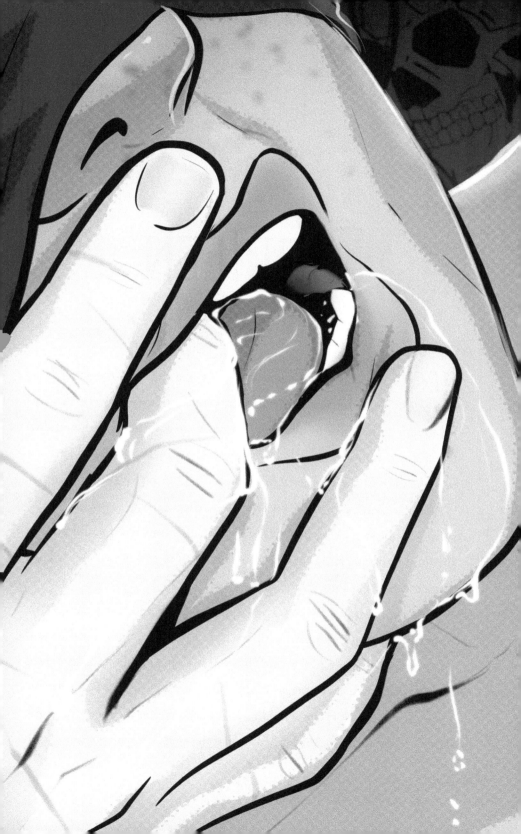

THIRTEEN

PERCY

To say I was nervous to move into the alpha frat with the other guys would be the understatement of the century. I knew it was necessary. I'd fought so hard for it, after all. But my visit with my dad there hung like a shadow above me as I shoved the last of my bags—cheap garbage ones—full of my shit under Stinky's bed. Well, mine for the moment.

Haden's jacket had received two of its own garbage bags, because I wasn't about to fucking play with that shit. It wasn't like I could pop by the local boutique and buy one to replace it, even though whatever faint scent it'd had was long gone.

Brett wasn't home, which I was grateful for because it gave me the opportunity to get familiar with the space. As I popped my pills and shoved them into the nightstand, I found myself super fucking grateful I had the ones they gave omegas in the military so they could fly under the radar. So that their cycles wouldn't affect them while they were on duty. They weren't really meant for people like me—people who had no reason to take them, other than the fear of their father's fury. That had never stopped me though.

I'd been thinking about them a lot lately.

Especially because there'd been this feeling eating away under my skin for the last few months, my blood thrumming too quickly through my veins, my toes and fingers tingling when they shouldn't be. My bond bite throbbed sometimes too, like it was echoing the call of *wrong, wrong, wrong* that danced inside my veins.

Maybe it was the suppressants.

Or maybe I was just drinking too much caffeine.

Percy: I got my stuff moved in

Tommy: Dude! Wtf

Percy: ?

Tommy: I was supposed to help you

Percy: Didn't need help

Tommy: I hate you sometimes 🙄

I snorted at my phone, a smile pulling at my lips as I flopped onto my mattress and watched Tommy's speech bubble blink in and out for several minutes. He'd offered to help cart my shit across campus when he was out of work, but I hadn't wanted to wait.

Waiting would mean delaying the inevitable, and I wasn't ready for that.

Tommy: Are you coming to my room tonight, or am I coming to yours?

I chewed on my lip. As much as I thought Brett was a pretty cool dude after the whole rescuing me from my dad thing—I couldn't forget the way he'd fucked with me to get Tommy's number. I didn't really know what would happen if Tommy decided to come over to the house—worried he'd start calling everyone dick-o-nauts, or force me to let him paint my toes again—so I figured it was better to keep those two sides of my life separate, even though I felt kinda shitty doing that to him.

Cut the woe-is-me bullshit, I chastised myself. Except talking to myself only made me feel more pathetic.

I felt pretty pathetic in general, actually, especially because I missed Tommy, even though I'd seen him literally two hours ago. He'd petted my head and fed me donuts, and I wasn't sure when the next time we'd get to do that would be. I wasn't sure I was worth the effort, even for the short trek across campus. When he showed up at my new house a few hours later carting a giant pizza box and a two-liter of Mountain Dew, huffing about having to walk all the way over, I knew we'd be alright.

Moving made me nervous, which I hadn't expected. I didn't do well with change, which became even more apparent as the months blurred together, winter becoming spring, becoming summer.

Living at my new house was normal enough. The guys steered clear of me for the most part like they always had. Not because they knew about me—Brett had sworn to me he wouldn't tell—but because I was a

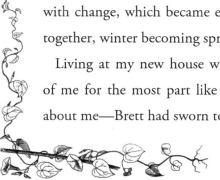

bit of a basket case nowadays. That itching feeling beneath my skin had only grown worse the more time had passed. That paired with my Dad's radio silence and the fact that my brother, Marv, had texted me at the beginning of the new semester and told me not to come home for a while till Dad cooled off, was enough to make me sick to my stomach pretty much all the freaking time.

At least Tommy and I were still solid, even though lately he'd been annoying me.

I'd worried about that, especially during those first weeks with us living on opposite sides of campus. Worried we'd drift apart like two logs floating down a stream. The more off-kilter I felt, the more I realized I still needed his sunshine in my life. It was really the only sunshine I had, other than my plants.

Work at the greenhouse was steady enough. Spring and summer were the busy months and I worked overtime with Mr. Becker most weekends. Sometimes Mrs. Becker would even pop by and feed us pizza, and that was kinda the highlight of my entire fucking life. Even if she did insist I use napkins, and brought like a gallon of hand sanitizer with her.

I liked the plants the most, but the Beckers were cool too.

Even though usually things were pretty good between us, even Tommy stressed me out sometimes. As much as his presence soothed me, he always had to throw in these random comments about the guys from the frat. He seemed to think Brett especially was hiding something, which I reassured him, more than once, couldn't be the case. Brett was a good dude. He hadn't batted an eye when I'd told him I was an omega. Hadn't treated me any different, other than to help me with my dad. I'd lived with him for months now and I'd never seen so much as a red flag outside of that thing last winter with Tommy's number.

It hadn't taken long for me to forgive that either, since Brett had apologized two weeks later. No one ever said sorry to me, so I'd been a bit blindsided, though appreciative.

Tommy was convinced he was lying, though, and it made it real fucking awkward sometimes. I didn't know what to do when he got all heated about it, so I just shut down and shut off. Let him talk his fill and tuned him out as I watched *The Office* reruns on his laptop, both of us cramped on his tiny bed, while I waited for him to stop.

On nights like those I'd head home, crawl beneath my blankets, and when I'd close my eyes, I'd wake up beside Haden.

Sometimes it felt like the twisted up feelings inside me were the reason I searched for him in my dreams. The more I visited him, the easier it became to do so again, my soul sifting through shadow till I caught the string of whatever bond bound us together and followed its path through the dark toward him.

Most of the time, Haden was in his office like he'd been the first time I'd visited. He'd glance up from his papers, push them aside, and greet me with a look that was both amused and tentative. Like he was surprised to see me, pleased too, but apprehensive.

He never spoke about his offer for me to stay though, even though he was always eager to touch.

Gods don't share their play things. That's what he'd murmured to me as I'd writhed in ecstasy, my body twisted up in his silken sheets. I didn't feel like much of a play thing, though, despite his words.

"Why?" Haden had asked once when I'd popped up beside him as he traipsed down a dark, candlelit hallway. I could hear the *click, clack skuttle*

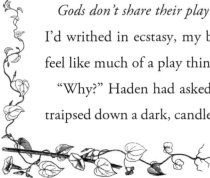

of *something* just around the bend, my pulse thrumming with fear as Haden caught a glimpse of the bandage I kept taped religiously over my bond mark, and quickly distracted me. Usually I'd wear a turtleneck too. Double layers of protection against prying eyes. I ignored the fact that I usually showed up naked when I visited him, that the bandage being present at all was an anomaly. Maybe something lurking behind the cage protecting my heart had wanted him to see.

To see the parts of me I was ashamed of and welcome me back anyway.

I knew he was a figment of my imagination, but I still sought his comfort.

Haden hadn't looked offended, just curious as he reached out to trace his thumb over the edge of the bandage. He was always so gentle, until he wasn't. The thought made me grin, and I'd shuddered, offering him my neck, the tingle of his fingertips soothing the itch beneath my skin.

"Why, what?" I'd played dumb.

"Are you ashamed?" he'd asked, and I hadn't known what to say. My answer was complicated.

Part of me was. But...an even deeper, more visceral part of me was protective, *possessive*. Like the bite was the first thing in this world that had been given to me, and me alone. It was *mine*. I didn't want to share it, not with anyone. So I just nodded and watched his eyes glimmer in the dark.

Still so inhuman, but familiar now.

"Liar," he'd teased, because we both knew my secret.

Things were great for the summer. Awesome even. My life was a puzzle

and for the first time, it felt like all the pieces were falling into place. The guys had finally warmed up to me. Brett and I had taken to starting our own binge watch of shitty sitcoms, and Tommy had stopped heckling me about alpha-holes, *hallelujah*.

I was still banished from Dad's place, but it didn't feel like much of a loss. Not when Marv kept me updated that Dad had been fired from his most recent job, and therefore had been on a bender since the beginning of July. I didn't really want to be under the line of fire, so I steered clear and worked at the greenhouse as often as possible to save up extra cash. Neither of my brothers attracted his attention the way I did, so I wasn't really worried about them, though I was relieved when they'd randomly update me so I'd know they weren't lying dead in a ditch somewhere.

Buck, my other older brother, sent me obscure memes he pulled from the internet every so often that made pretty much no sense to anyone but him, so I figured despite Dad being angry at me, my brothers and I were still chill.

I was doing well in my classes now that the fall semester started. Which was wild, considering the fact I'd never been good at school. I was a straight C student most of my life, which had been a problem, but now that I was in college, it didn't seem to matter. C's meant passing and that was good enough. I'd had a final on my birthday, but it hadn't really mattered. I didn't celebrate. I never had.

It just wasn't how we did things, though Tommy somehow had extorted my birthday out of me, so I shouldn't have been surprised when I showed up to my new room and my bed had a six pack of Mountain Dew sitting on my pillow along with a chocolate cake that I squirreled away to snack on while the rest of the guys were asleep.

Maybe it was the cake that made me feel sick later, or maybe it was that same growing itchiness under my skin. Either way, I woke up late that night. With the house in silence, the creaking of the floorboards echoed ominously through the air. They always got noisy after dark, like with the world quiet the house was trying to speak.

My throat was dry and my head was foggy as I rose groggily from bed, sparing a glance across the room to the lump on Brett's bed where he lay sleeping.

Except.

He wasn't there.

I shrugged off my unease, forcing myself out of the bedroom as quietly as I could, dodging laundry baskets and wayward solo cups as I made my way down the loud-as-fuck wooden hallway and wandered down the stairs in search of water.

There was a light on in the kitchen and warning bells began to ring in the back of my head as I paused when I got to the bottom of the landing, something sitting not quite right. When I glanced down at my phone, I noted the time. Two a.m.

Huh.

I could hear the murmur of voices, so I crept closer, my heartbeat fluttering as my palms began to slick with sweat. This…wasn't normal. No, normally—I was invited to any and all parties. Even when I'd been in a rut, I'd still always been offered at least an invitation. It was a bit weird, though, that lately my frat brothers had all been nicer than normal.

Maybe that should've clued me in that something was wrong.

But I hadn't wanted to listen to Tommy's doom and gloom. (See? He's the one that's a pessimist!) So I'd ignored it, just figured it was the world finally righting itself after so long of giving me absolute shit.

I supposed if I *hadn't* been invited to this weird middle-of-the-night-kitchen-party, it was my own fault, probably.

I'd been going to sleep earlier and earlier lately, and after I'd plowed through an entire cake on my own, I'd passed out pretty much immediately. Most days, by the time the sun went down, the exhaustion hit me like a ton of bricks, with or without cake. No amount of caffeine seemed able to remedy the situation either, that itchy feeling under my skin only amplifying when I was at my absolute worst.

I crept closer, finally catching the tail end of someone's words as my heart sank somewhere beneath my feet.

"Last time he left the house, I went through his nightstand and you wouldn't believe what I found."

That was Brett talking. We'd been hanging out enough lately there was no way I wouldn't recognize his voice, even from a distance. Dude had a major skater-dude accent when he was with anyone but me. Like he thought talking that way would help him pick up omegas, or impress the other alphas at the house.

They all kinda did that though, postured with each other, put up these fronts to appear cool. I couldn't blame them for that though, because it wasn't like I was being honest with any of them either.

"What?" That was Frank. Deeper voice. Scratchier too.

"Fucking…" Brett paused for what I assumed to be dramatic effect. That sinking feeling inside me only grew stronger, like a black hole sucking me

132

deep, deep down into the unknown. "*Suppressants.*"

I could practically see the nefarious jazz-hands he was probably wielding.

The way he said suppressants made it sound like it was a bad word. Scandalous. Something to be ashamed of. Which, realistically, I knew it was. I wasn't supposed to be taking them. Hell, I was never supposed to be taking them. The fact that I'd gotten a prescription for them in the first place was because the doctor who prescribed them was willfully negligent. Everyone knew that. That's why he was my dad's favorite. A secret weapon to get pain meds and blockers whenever the fuck he wanted.

"Really?" Frank sounded equal parts dubious and delighted. I knew they were talking about me. It didn't take a genius to figure that out, since I was pretty damn sure there wasn't another dude at the frat pretending not to be an omega. But *still,* something inside me hoped they weren't. Prayed, they weren't, even though I'd never been one for prayers.

"Dude's all blanked up."

I flinched, acid climbing up my throat at the slur. Blanked up. Something I'd heard alphas laugh about for years, but never heard directed at me. To be an omega that was blanked up meant you were practically worthless, even though that wasn't how suppressants worked. No pheromones. No senses. No way to attract a mate with your systems all blank.

"It's a shame, honestly." Brett laughed. "He gives off the biggest 'fuck me' vibes I've ever seen. Like a deer or something. Ready to get run over." He laughed again and the sick feeling only amplified.

"With your dick!" Frank cackled.

Fuck me eyes.

Why did everyone say that about me?

It still hadn't hit me yet that this conversation meant Brett had spilled

my secret. That he'd lied to me. They all had. I didn't want to believe it was true, forcing the feelings to the back of my mind as I continued to listen, praying I'd find out they were talking about someone else, anyone else. Even if that made me a shitty person. Wishing someone else was getting disrespected like this.

Brett quieted and, for a moment, I thought that was it. That the worst had happened already. That my thoughts weren't spaghetti. That I wasn't about to shatter. And then he spoke again, and I nearly threw up all over my hole-ridden socks.

"Wonder if he still gets slick," Brett groaned, the sound playfully pornographic. "*Fuck.* I was after his roommate before he moved in, but a hole's a hole, right? Who cares if he's not pretty, so long as he's got a tight ass."

I stumbled back, disgust and alarm blaring inside my head, my earlier thirst forgotten. The adrenaline pumping through my veins sent me into a tailspin as I bumped against the banister and tried to breathe through my rising panic.

Wonder if he still gets slick.

A hole's a hole.

Who cares if he's not pretty?

Spinning, spinning, *spinning.*

Bile rose and my damp palms trembled as the laughter in the other room paused.

"What was that?" Frank again. Fuck. I'd hit the bannister too hard. I held still for a moment, my breathing ragged, my teeth bared. I wanted to go back upstairs. To fall asleep. To fall into the darkness and tear my way to where Haden slept at the back of my mind. He'd comfort me, even if

134

he wasn't really mine. Even if he wasn't really real.

"Probably just the stairs being creaky as fuck again," Brett replied.

Spinning, spinning, *spinning*.

"Don't remind me. Last time I tried to sneak someone home, I got clocked by fucking Matthews the second he heard them squeaking."

"Fuck you, dude." Matthews replied, followed by the sound of a scuffle. "I didn't say shit."

"Whatever." Frank was laughing, and the laughter sounded fake to me. Nothing felt real. Like the world was made of plastic and it was melting beneath my feet.

I don't know how, but somehow I made it up to my room in one piece. I could still hear Brett and Frank's laughter echoing through the back of my mind as I lay with my blanket over my head, my hands shaking. I wanted to text Tommy, but I didn't. I already knew what he'd say. He'd warned me about this. Warned me a thousand times. I just…I *couldn't*. I was too tired.

Too fucking tired.

I wanted to escape.

I wanted comfort.

I wanted *Haden*.

Sleep, I commanded myself.

Sleep.

Please—

God. I refused to cry. Pathetic. Fucking pathetic. I squeezed my eyes shut tight, forcing myself to breathe through my nostrils as my hands shook and my stomach churned.

Sleep, sleep, sleep, *sleep*.

FOURTEEN

HADEN

He was back again. I could sense his presence as his soul flickered to life a few feet in front of my desk. I steeled myself, my words already prepared as I pushed my paperwork to the side and caught the faint traces of sugar on his skin.

"You can't keep coming here." My voice was steady. Steadier than I felt.

Percy's hands flexed, clenching into fists, his big body quaking. He was dressed this time. Fully dressed. The shirt he wore was slick with sweat, his loose gray pants covered in years old stains, the hems full of holes.

"I can't help it." His words were nothing but a quiet, broken breath.

"You are the one crossing between realms, not me." I reminded him.

I doubted he understood what he was doing at all. In fact, I wouldn't be surprised if he thought this was all a dream, that his visits here weren't as real as the visit I'd taken to the surface when I'd first met him.

"I can't—" There was a hurt quality to his words, like a cornered animal, but still, I refused to look him in the eye. I knew I'd give in to him the moment I did, and it was better for us both if we ended things now, before it was too late.

For months, I'd picked apart crumbs of knowledge till I'd come to my current conclusion.

"You do not realize the danger," I spoke candidly. It was true. He had no idea what the lasting effects of soul wandering were. He had no idea that the bond between us grew stronger with every trip to my realm. That his body lay empty back in his world full of humans and laughter—and experiences I could never give him here.

His soul was missing.

Like it always was at night when he searched for me.

His body, a lifeless husk left behind unprotected.

I knew this. I'd known this for months after some extensive research of my own. And yet…for months, I had not been able to bring myself to send him away. I'd feasted on his pleasure, became familiar with the way he sobbed, the way he begged—though I'd somehow refrained from fucking him again. A miracle considering the fact he made me weak in a way that was not becoming of a king.

"Haden, please." Such sweet words. Like candied sugar spinning round and around.

I couldn't give in.

Not this time.

It was for his own good. *And mine*, I added privately. I couldn't keep going like this. Couldn't keep seeing him, tasting him, touching him. Couldn't let him continue to wake up the parts of me I'd killed. Couldn't let him thaw the last frozen bits of my heart. He *couldn't* stay. He wouldn't. He didn't belong here.

He belonged beneath the sun, where wild things grew, and young puppies like him could frolic with endless possibility at the tips of their fingers. He belonged between colorful bodies full of life. Mistakes yet to be made. Sins yet to be punished.

I could not offer him that here.

That was why I'd come to this conclusion, one I didn't want to make. An ultimatum I didn't want to give.

"Enough, Percy."

His fists clenched again. He was trembling all over, the scent of his sweat tingling inside my nose. I rarely used his name, just like he rarely used mine. It was a boundary we didn't cross. Pet names were easier, though no less personal.

"You haven't made the choice to stay. Therefore I cannot help you anymore." We'd run out of time weeks ago but I'd been weak. So fucking weak for those big hazel eyes and abused pink lips. Weak for the smile he so rarely graced me with. Weak for the way he picked apart my library, disgusted by the complicated texts. Weak for the way he marveled at the simplest things. I knew my voice was trembling, but I couldn't stop it, couldn't stop the emotion from breaking the surface.

He didn't speak.

Because I was apparently a masochist, I finally let myself look at his face.

I shouldn't have.

But even in this, I was powerless to refuse him.

Percy's eyes were glassy, the dark circles beneath them so bruised he looked nearly beaten. Splotchy red cheeks. A scab bisecting his bottom lip where it had been abused so beautifully it bled. His temples were slick with sweat, his tawny brown hair matted to his scalp. He shook. All over.

Large shoulders trembling, his chest heaving with each needy shudder for air. In, and out. Suffering, so beautifully. But the satisfaction I normally felt when I saw him like this was missing because it had not been my hand that had caused it.

I gave in.

"Oh, darling. What have they done to you now?" The pet name slipped out, but I couldn't bring myself to regret the words as Percy's shoulders collapsed and he stumbled his way toward me immediately. I patted my lap, and despite the fact that we were nearly the same size, he didn't hesitate as he climbed atop my thighs and buried his trembling face in the hollow beside my neck.

I could feel his shaking now more than I could see it, smoothing my hands down his back, petting over the muscle in a way he so rarely let me.

"Please, alpha." Percy's lips trembled against the side of my neck.

He was heavy and warm. I nuzzled into his sweaty temple, inhaling greedily, chasing the faint traces of his scent hiding somewhere beneath chemical blankness.

"Please." To my surprise Percy released me. He sank to his knees, his broad shoulders forcing my legs wide to accommodate as he settled beneath my desk, staring up at me with those eyes…the eyes that made me want to burn the world down, just to make him smile. He nuzzled the inside of my knee, needy. *Sweet.*

I threaded my fingers through his hair, scratching at his scalp as a shuddered exhale left his lips.

He wanted to forget.

It had been months since he'd asked this of me.

Instead, our days had been spent quietly conversing, his cock in my

mouth, or vice versa. Sex had quickly become his favorite way to let go, and I had indulged him, probably more than was healthy. But when he asked me for something, I found it nearly impossible to say no.

I was supposed to be creating distance between us now.

I had already decided it was time to let him go.

But...

"Help me forget," Percy begged, just like I'd thought he would. The words were forced, painful and sharp.

"This isn't healthy for either of us," I reminded him gently, even though his close proximity to my cock made it impossible to ignore how much I wanted him.

"I need it." That same hurt quality to his voice was back, that same glassy, lost look on his face. Like he was searching for religion between my thighs. Desperate for kindness. I had never been a kind being. I'd been chosen for this job because of my casual indifference, or so I thought. But he brought out things inside me I hadn't even known existed.

"I don't want to hurt you," I brushed a thumb over a stray eyelash that had fallen on his cheek, and he shuddered at the innocent touch. One more time would only deepen the bond between us.

"You're hurting me right now."

God. Those words. A sudden lancing pain tore through my heart and I knew in that moment, there was no way I could deny him. I was too weak. I'd always been expected to be strong, always excelled at putting up walls. But with those simple words, every wall I'd built around myself crumbled to the ground. My fortresses no longer fortified.

"Please, I just..." Percy trailed off, searching my gaze. I was glad of the barrier between us, the last one. My mask had somehow stayed on the

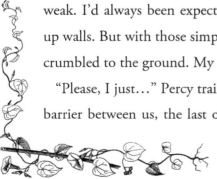

140

entire time we'd been together, the last remaining protection between us. "I need it." He shook so beautifully. "I need *you.*"

And who was I to deny him?

A god who worshiped a mortal.

I gave his head another gentle scratch, tracing up behind the shell of his sensitive pink ears, watching his lashes flutter as he relaxed fractionally. He was too raw right now. No matter what he said. Sex wasn't the correct answer. He needed…something else. Something that would make him feel useful. Something to give him purpose.

"I have to finish my paperwork," I lied, a quiet rumble in the space between us. "Can you wait?"

Maybe I was testing him.

Testing his devotion.

Percy passed with flying colors, nodding in relief, his shoulders slumping in relief now that I was no longer actively pushing him away. He nuzzled at the inside of my knee gratefully, like simply allowing him to be close like this was the greatest gift I could give him.

For a while, I let him sit there.

He never stopped chasing my scent with his nose, rubbing along the fabric of my trousers, his lashes wet, brow furrowed. I knew he found my lack of scent just as frustrating as I found his. Minutes passed. An hour. I worked my way through exactly zero of my documents, too distracted by the omega between my legs. Broad shouldered, with the faint scent of his slick beginning to waft in the air between us.

Percy mouthed at the fabric of my pants, sucking it into his mouth, tasting the texture with his tongue. He couldn't seem to help himself. He was always happiest with something in his mouth.

"You have an oral fixation unlike anything I've ever seen," I told him softly, my free hand still carding through his hair. He blinked up at me, a foggy peace having settled across his features. His earlier trembling had quieted, though he seemed unable to sit completely still. "I have an idea."

He perked up, clearly excited for whatever I was about to give him.

I could practically see his hypothetical tail wagging.

I suppose that was fair, when I'd been ready to give him exactly nothing just an hour ago.

"I don't know what that means," Percy replied honestly, docile eyes blinking up at me. A pretty little rabbit, caught between my paws. Maybe this was why Gods weren't supposed to interact with the mortals. One look from those hazel eyes and here I was, tossing all my resolve out the window just to please him.

Even though I knew it would only hurt us both.

I undid the buckle on my belt, letting the leather slip free, the quiet sound of it *snicking* free unnaturally loud in the quiet room. I hoped we wouldn't be interrupted. Normally my head advisor Bertram would knock before entering—he and all the others who resided in the palace liked to matchmake whenever Percy came round, despite never actually seeing him—but I figured with Percy hidden neatly under the desk there was no harm in a little…play.

I stroked the cold buckle across the swell of his cheekbone and watched him shudder. Percy gasped, so I repeated the motion on the other side, watching his eyes cross as he tried to follow the belt's movement. I trailed it across his square jawline, not too sharp, softened at the edges. Like he still had baby fat to lose despite being all man. I wondered if he would always look this way. Young. Naive.

Desperate.

Stroking the buckle down the center of his neck, I bit back a growl as his Adam's apple bobbed and a trail of goosebumps rose in the metal's wake.

Flicking the button on my pants open made Percy lick his lips, his attention immediately gravitating to the trail of white hair that crept beneath the edge of my black undergarments.

"You're going to suck my cock, Percy." I told him, a mirror of what I'd said all those months ago. If this was to be our last time, I needed him to remember it. "And you are going to like it."

"I thought you said no sex until after you finished?" Percy perked up, though his thick brows remained twisted in confusion. His response was so cute I couldn't help but count the freckles that dusted the bridge of his scrunched up nose with affection.

"This isn't sex," I told him, delighted when I watched his eyes narrow suspiciously. He was dubious, and I couldn't blame him. I shouldn't love to play with his feelings like this. Like a cat batting its paw in a fishbowl just to watch the fish inside swim in circles.

"How is sucking your cock not sex?" Percy glared at me.

"I suppose *sucking* is the wrong word," I murmured, reaching down to tuck the elastic of my boxers beneath my balls. My cock gave an eager twitch but I willed it to softness, watching the way Percy's eyes grew dark and that sweet pink tongue flickered out to wet his lips once again. "You're going to *hold* my cock in your mouth."

"Just...hold it?" He blinked up at me.

"You may suck if you wish. But don't get me hard."

Percy still looked dubious, but it was clear he wasn't going to argue, too eager to take whatever I'd give him, even if he didn't understand it.

"Keep it warm, pup," I murmured quietly, before promising, "You'll like it."

Percy seemed to contemplate this. For almost a full minute, I watched warring emotions flit across his face. Desire, confusion, desire again. Until finally, he let the last of his inhibitions go and eagerly leaned forward, mouth open.

The first touch of his lips against my cock should not have made me gasp.

I bit my lip, then released it, forcing myself to remain stoic as Percy's sweet pink lips wrapped around the tip of my soft dick experimentally. It jerked beneath his touch, and that movement seemed to bolster him forward, despite my command not to get me hard. He stared up at me through his lashes, a look of concentration on his face as he opened wider and let my cock slide along the slippery-hot caress of his tongue.

Wet. Hot. Tight.

Heaven.

I let him get used to it, stroking over his head as he settled, gently suckling. The longer he held me steady the more the renewed tension in his body began to bleed away as a foggy fucked-out expression overtook his handsome face.

"Better?" I murmured, unable to help myself as I thumbed over his upper lip, watching the way it threatened to twitch into a smile. His mouth was so warm, comforting almost. I hadn't expected to like receiving this as much as I'd liked ordering him to do it. But it was most definitely pleasant. Too bad I wouldn't get to do it again.

"Mmmm." Percy hummed his agreement around me and the thrum of his voice made my eyes nearly roll back. I forced myself not to react,

willing my cock to stay soft as I turned back to my paperwork with a quiet hum.

"I thought so."

At first, it was hard to focus with his mouth around me. The way Percy eagerly suckled was so innocent and vulgar all at once. The way his drool dripped down my balls, his sweet little nose huffing away as he inhaled my scent directly from the source. *Greedy as always.*

He didn't try to clean himself up either. He just sucked and drooled, seemingly content to let me do my work now that he had something in his mouth to play with.

Despite my resolve not to get hard, I couldn't help the way my cock twitched every so often, like it wanted to remind Percy of how good he was being. Obedient. Sweet.

After I'd gotten somewhat used to the sensation, it was easier to work. In a strange way, Percy's quiet focus made my own easier to grasp. I whipped through my last pages of paperwork easily, my focus only wavering every so often so I could look down and check on him between my legs.

I didn't think I'd ever seen him so content.

There was this dazed look in his eyes that made him appear peaceful and happy, like there was nowhere else in the world he'd rather be than on his knees with my dick in his mouth.

Finally, I pushed the last of my work aside, twisting to look at him again, before I gave his hair a gentle pull to remind him who was calling the shots.

"Are you still hungry, pet?" I murmured, my dick hardening inside the tight clutch of his mouth as he blinked prettily up at me, his big thighs spread wide, the view of the slope of his muscular back all the way to his

meaty ass more than a little obscene from my angle.

My fangs itched.

Percy whined, this long needy sound that had my hair standing on end and my cock standing to attention. Well, *that* answered that. We both knew I wasn't talking about food.

All it took was a single glance to see that Percy was hard, his sweatpants tented eagerly, a wet spot leaking through the fabric where the fat head of his dick pressed tight. With sudden clarity, I realized he wasn't wearing undergarments. All that stood between that wanton little cock and his pleasure was a flimsy piece of too-old fabric.

I'd been a king for longer than I could remember, but until that moment I'd never truly known what it meant to have everything.

"I can smell your slick, you know?" I murmured, wishing I had a better view of his ass. Wishing I could see if the back of his pants were as slick with his pleasure as the front.

Percy groaned low, the sound vibrating my balls and making my hips shift in an aborted fuck upward. Gods, he drove me out of my mind. Made me want to chase him. Bite him. Plow him on every available surface till his slick dripped down my sac and his cum decorated my kingdom.

"Your body calls to me," I murmured, aware I was digging my own grave. "More honest than even you are."

Leaning down, I cradled the back of Percy's head, stroking along his fragile skull with purpose. My hips fucked forward again and this time I didn't stop them, letting my sac slap against his wet chin as his lashes fluttered and he struggled to keep my growing length inside his mouth.

"*Fuck me, fuck me, Haden,*" I teased, pulling back to fuck forward again. "That's what your slick begs." *Slap, slap, slap.* He whined. "Fuck my wet

146

little hole." *Fuuuck.* He sucked me down, slick and eager, the blunt edges of his teeth scraping a little along my cock, though I didn't stop. I couldn't. "*I'm so hungry.*"

The noise Percy made then was the neediest thing I'd ever heard. Like he agreed with me. Like my words were just a tease, and he was begging me to follow through. I could see his cock bobbing, his own pleasure obvious, though his hands remained on top of his thighs rather than touch where we both knew he wanted to. They squeezed, and released, nails bunching up the fabric as he focused on servicing me, rather than his own pleasure..

The more he enjoyed pleasing me, the more I enjoyed fucking him.

I couldn't help the way I ground against his face, panting, a needy growl rumbling in my chest.

This was the last time.

The last time I'd let him touch me like this.

The last time I'd feel the warmth of his mouth, see the way his eyes grew distant and peaceful like they only did when he had a cock inside him. The last time I'd twist my fingers in his hair and let myself become the man I knew I must've been before I'd been chosen.

The last time I'd let him use me as a way to forget the monsters on his side of the world.

The last time I'd become a monster for him.

It was the last time, and it never should've happened at all.

"Why can't I say no to you?" My moan was mournful as I emptied myself down his throat, more than a little dazed and appreciative as I watched him swallow every last drop, eyes pinched shut with enthusiasm. He didn't even gag. His tongue was hot and eager as he released me, lapping at the soft skin of my sac, tasting the salt of my skin as he licked me clean.

Percy's eyes were dazed as I soothed him, stroking through his hair, carding my fingers through it till his face scrunched up with pleasure and his swollen lips tipped into a sated sunny smile. The wet spot on the front of his pants made it clear he'd come at the same time I had.

He was *perfect*.

Resilient and stubborn.

Sweet.

Too good for me, for the life I could give him.

"You can't come here again, pet." I murmured, softer this time.

He didn't understand why, so he just blinked, thinking—like always—I would give in to him. But I couldn't. Any longer here and the tether between his soul and his body would sever. *I could keep him here*, a dark part of my mind supplied, my possessive heart fluttering. He wouldn't know the difference.

But the idea of letting his body waste away, rotting wherever he'd lain his head for the night made my stomach churn.

For someone who lived and breathed death, the idea of Percy's body dying made me sick.

Our bond was too strong. The bond neither of us had wanted. The bond I hadn't realized I could even initiate till it was too late, and I had been too selfish to let him go. The string that tied our souls glowed brightly as Percy reached with fumbling fingers and gently guided my now soft dick back into his mouth for one last leisurely suck. I shuddered, squeezing my eyes tight because I knew if I looked down at him even one more time, I would be ready to go again.

Don't look, I reminded myself.

But I looked anyway. I could feel the way Percy whined around me before dropping his face to nuzzle the inside of my thigh again, the open air cold where it kissed my cock in stark contrast to the heat of his mouth. He was shaking all over again, like he'd only now remembered why he'd come to me in the first place, and I was *weak.* I was weak because I took him to bed. I tucked him inside my sheets and I plied him with my pillows.

Soon, he fell asleep beside me, and I stroked over his cheek and the swell of his flushed pink ears, knowing it was the last time I would allow myself to indulge.

"It isn't safe," I murmured quietly, watching the way his eyelids fluttered and the tension in his body stayed far, far away. *Good.* At least if I couldn't keep him, I could give him this last gift.

You could keep him, my traitorous mind offered again.

He's miserable up there.

He calls it a nightmare.

He could be happy here.

With you.

Percy's skin was soft as I memorized the pattern of his freckles and the moles that danced between the swell of his pecs. There were cigarette burns littered here and there beside other random scars. I smoothed over them with my fingers in apology before venturing north again. Pink nipples hardened beneath the brush of my palm and his breath stuttered when I stroked down his sternum, tracing his ribs, and grabbing his hip tight enough to bruise.

Breathing hurt.

My chest was tight.

My lungs squeezed.

I didn't hug him.

That was one step too far.

A leap I couldn't—*wouldn't* make.

And when it was clear there was no other choice left, I closed my eyes and searched for the string that tied us. It burst with light, bright as a summer day, the bond well fed, our tether glorious. I hesitated. Its warmth filled my chest with pleasure. But the hesitation lasted for only a moment. Long enough I could imagine a life where I could keep him. A world where the living could commune with the dead, the line between us nonexistent. But that was just a fantasy, and though I was a god—a selfish one—I knew I couldn't take this from him.

The things that made his heart beat.

I couldn't take away his sun.

By not choosing me, he'd made his choice.

So I severed the tie between us, watching as it frayed and frayed, fragments breaking off and floating away like spiderwebs. When it was done, I felt emptier than I ever had before. Only darkness remained and when I opened my eyes, Percy was gone, the indent in the mattress beside me the only indication he'd ever been there at all.

Ah.

Regret.

An emotion I'd hoped I'd never feel again, but here we were.

I closed my eyes and slept.

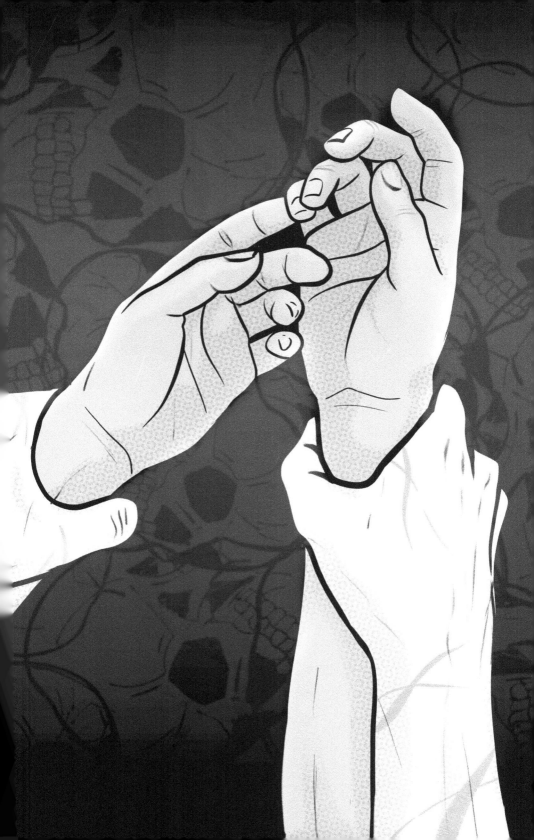

FIFTEEN

PERCY

Haden was gone.

I knew it the moment I woke up alone in the darkness. Before that moment, I hadn't realized he'd been with me at all—that his presence had crept under the surface of my skin. It had been a balm over the itchiness that ached through my body, soothing some of the exhaustion and pain that had consistently plagued me for months. Without him there I was left reeling, the sickness that had built inside me welling up like it meant to drown me.

Deeper and deeper I sank.

The more helpless I felt, the darker the water became.

Brett slept peacefully in his bed beside mine, and when I looked at his face, I nearly didn't recognize him. His words from just hours ago seemed a world away, though they hitched a ride in my heart beside all the other injustices I'd swallowed over the years.

I was stupid.

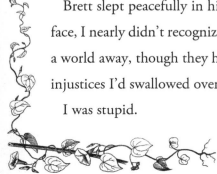

A stupid omega.

Stupid enough I hadn't seen what was right under my nose all along.

And now I was alone.

As time passed, the sickness only grew worse. Days turned to weeks, into months. The brisk autumn turned cruel as the first lick of winter crept up on the sleeping town of Madison. During those bitter months, I spent as much time as I could away from my roommates, terrified of what would happen should my guard drop, should the sickness consume me entirely.

Living with demons should've been familiar.

But the sickness only made everything worse.

Still, I reasoned it away.

Figured it had something to do with the loss of Haden in my life. The hole he'd left behind, figment of my imagination or not, was gaping and raw. It seeped into everything I did, the memory of his quiet embrace, of the way he'd made me feel more like myself than I ever had before.

Without him, I felt like a shadow.

I'd always felt that way, so it shouldn't have hurt as much as it did to become invisible again. But I knew what it felt like to let go of my inhibitions. To be who I could've been instead of who I was raised to be.

I should've admitted to Tommy what had happened. Should've told him about Brett. Told him about Haden. I should've done a lot of things. Instead, I drank a shit-ton more caffeine, pounded through my last classes of the semester, and ignored the gaping black hole in my chest that threatened to swallow me whole.

I started losing time.

A few minutes.

An hour.

Two.

The more time I lost, the more frightened I became of what could happen to me when I got like that. My apathy shifted into fear every time I woke up, unaware of what day it was, or where I was. That was when I knew there was something fundamentally wrong with me. That I should ask for help. If anyone else had been in the same situation I was in, that would've been what I recommended. But…I was just too fucking tired to care.

Eventually, when the weakness grew to be too much, my guard lowered, my body too sick to expend energy on anything other than hiding my illness—I took to sleeping in the greenhouse. It was warm there. Safe too. There was this steady *beep, beep* that buzzed any time the door to the building was opened, so I knew I'd have some warning if anyone tried to disturb me.

No one noticed, thank god, even though I knew Mr. and Mrs. Becker suspected when they'd catch me with dirt in my hair, shoving blankets into the cupboard at the back of the break room. They didn't say anything, though.

I'd been spending a lot of time there since summer, more than usual, searching for happiness between the leaves of plants, stroking along petals and looking for peace. At night I lay on my back, my head cradled on a bag of soft soil, a blanket tucked around my body as I breathed in the soothing scent of earth and wondered why things couldn't be different. The stars were as foggy as my thoughts.

I'd been running for so long from myself I didn't know what to do now that I'd had a taste of what I could be.

Potential was bittersweet.

That night I got to the greenhouse later than usual. It had been hard to slip out of the frat house unnoticed, but I'd managed. I was only supposed to rest here for a few hours. The morning shift would be out wandering the aisles in a few short hours and I needed to be packed up and ready to act normal by then. But everything felt murky around the edges, the world faded and twisted. Even lifting my head felt like too much effort.

I could taste Haden on my tongue and I chased it, following the darkness inside me, searching for the glimmer of light that had tethered me to him for so long.

It's not safe. That's what he'd said.

But like always, he'd been a cryptic son-of-a-bitch, so he hadn't told me *what* wasn't safe.

Maybe he thought I was too stupid to understand, like everyone else did. But…I knew that wasn't it. Haden wasn't hateful. I didn't need to see his face to know that. He had a kind sort of confidence, though his kindness was tentative. Like it was a muscle he wasn't used to flexing. I could relate. I hoped he was okay, wherever he was.

It felt weird to worry about someone other than me. Maybe I was a selfish son-of-a-bitch myself. Before I'd met him, all I'd ever been concerned with was my own survival. I wasn't afraid to fight tooth and nail for it, unconcerned with who I left behind.

My head was so heavy.

Haden's jacket was a familiar weight on my chest.

I knew I should get up.

Survival dictated I open my eyes.

But I just…*couldn't.* The last bits of my strength leached into the chilled concrete floor. Somewhere out there was my alpha. And he was just as

alone as I was. Maybe even more so. He'd pushed me away. Cast me aside. But he hadn't been cruel, just...*sad.*

Like I was now.

"Dude, are you okay?" There was someone shaking me, but struggling toward the surface was more difficult than anything I'd ever done. Waterlogged from the inside out, I forced a ragged breath. *Where was I again?*

Humid. Warm. Soil.

Right.

The scents were flickering inside my nose, stronger than they'd ever been before. Overwhelming. I managed to get my eyes open, searching the room for the stranger whose scent made the inside of my nose burn. She kept shaking me, whoever she was. Her nails dug in, a bit of desperation creeping into her tone. "*Dude—*"

Right.

I needed to answer.

The world was a blur of colors. The woman who was shaking me had her red hair twisted back, little tendrils falling in her face. Distantly, I recognized her as the new part-timer we'd hired last month. I wasn't sure I'd said more than five words to her since she'd started working at the greenhouse.

"I'm okay." I blinked. The words came out all warped and wrong. I chased her scent, but it was wrong too. Too strong. Too sharp. Too—everything.

"You don't look okay," she fretted, though thankfully she stopped shaking me. "Shit." She twisted her hands together, lips pressed into a thin line. She was cute. An omega like me. But there was nothing wrong

with her, like there was with me. "I've got a car out back—I'll tell Chenise I'm taking you to the clinic."

Ah. I'd forgotten that was Mrs. Becker's first name. Then her words hit— The clinic.

The medical facility on campus. That was where I usually got my suppressants from, dutifully filling my prescription every three months. I'd avoided everything else about it—no check ups. Nothing. I hadn't felt like I needed it. Getting sick was for people with money. Now though…I wasn't so sure staying away had been a good idea.

It took the entire drive to the clinic for me to realize that I'd recognized her designation by scent. I hadn't been able to do that in years. Sure, I could infer—by a person's demeanor, body type, and general personality. There were exceptions, always, but for the most part, you could sense what someone was without having to literally scent them.

But I'd recognized her right away.

Dread sat like a pit in my stomach.

"I'll wait here for you," the redhead said. I wished I could remember her name. But I couldn't. Hell. That wasn't the only thing I'd been forgetting lately. When was the last time I'd taken my suppressants and blockers? I couldn't remember.

"I'm good." I waved her off, but she just glared at me till I conceded. *Fine.*

There were purple flowers lining the front of the building. It took me a second too long to realize they were fake, as was the grass. Their petals were the same color as the smattering of scars I'd seen decorating Haden's throat and across his jaw. I swallowed the homesickness that bubbled up inside me as the thought of him made me weary. The chime above the door sounded as I pushed my way weakly through, lost in morose thoughts.

Ding, ding.

I'm here, motherfuckers.

Maybe I was out of my mind. Maybe Haden hadn't even been real at all. Maybe this sickness was all in my head, something I made up to fill the emptiness inside me. Something to douse over my shadows, an artificial light to doctor the truth.

The redhead waited with me till it was my turn to go back, then gave me a friendly wave that I didn't have the energy to return as I disappeared into the exam room, Haden's jacket clenched tightly in my hands.

"Percy, right?" The doctor held her hand out to me, her expression gentle, though I could tell she kept it carefully blank. She could probably see how close I was to just saying *fuck this* to the whole thing and forcing my way out into the hallway. "I'm Dr. Reynolds."

I knew her name.

We'd met before, for my original exam before starting college. She was one of the few people on campus who *knew* about me. Obviously I was aware I shouldn't be a dick to her, even though I kinda wanted to, so I just waved half-heartedly and said, "Hi."

Dad never liked doctors.

Not ones he couldn't manipulate, anyway.

I swallowed the lump in my throat. Somehow I knew something bad was about to happen, though I didn't know what.

The last time I'd felt like this was the day before mom had died. Storm clouds on the horizon. Anxiety brewing like thunder in the distance.

"Why don't you have a seat, Percy?" Dr. Reynolds gestured at the crinkly paper-covered bench of shame and I glared at it before climbing on top, my cheeks burning with mortification.

The paper crunched beneath me as I shifted, rubbing my sweaty hands on my thighs. The fabric chafed against my slick palms. Everything around me was still a bit spinny, but the adrenaline in my veins was a balm for my sickness, apparently. The more anxious I got the easier it was to ignore it. I eyed her warily, unsure how to proceed.

"It says here on the chart you filled out that you've been experiencing dizziness, loss of time, and lethargy." She flipped to the back of the chart with a frown. "Is that correct?"

I didn't really want to admit it out loud. All laid out like that it sounded *bad*. So I just forced myself to nod, trying not to stare too hard at the giant diagrams of human anatomy on the wall. There was a drawing showing a dissected illustration of an omegas reproductive system and just looking at it made my skin crawl.

Was that really what I looked like inside? Gross.

"When did you start experiencing these feelings?"

My cheeks burned. "A couple months ago?" I felt stupid. Stupid for waiting this long to get help. Stupid for asking at all. I was just tired. That was it. Tired and missing my alpha, though I wasn't even sure my alpha was real at all.

I couldn't remember the last time I'd changed the bandage on my neck, terrified I'd peel it off only to see that Haden's teeth were no longer there. That I'd made it all up.

"Is this your first time visiting the clinic for this?" Reynolds asked gently, even though we both knew she already knew the answer to that.

"It wasn't necessary." I pulled out the big words, trying not to sound like I was about to be sick all over the crinkly, horrible table.

She was silent for a long, awkward moment before she nodded, wrote something down, and asked me another stupid question. "Has this ever happened to you before?"

"No," I bit out. I hadn't come here to play twenty questions, but I bit my tongue. Now that I was here I might as well see it through.

"Any recent changes in your life I should know about? New medications? Stressful events? Family issues?" *Nosy much? Jee-sus.*

Why did I come here?

Why did any of this matter?

I shook my head, more than a little miffed.

Maybe if I left now I wouldn't have to pay, seeing as how she hadn't done shit yet.

"Alright." Reynolds nodded, and I ignored the way the light caught her glasses and made her look like she had no eyes. Or I tried to anyway. I felt unsettled, but then again, I hadn't felt settled since the last time I'd seen Haden, so fuck me, I guess.

His jacket lay bunched up in my lap. I was a little ashamed to admit how quickly I'd started carrying it around. Clutching it close, chasing his scent with a desperation that made even me sick of myself. It hadn't taken long to stop hiding it, despite my earlier reservations. It was now a permanent fixture on my body at all times.

"Alright, thank you for answering my questions, Percy." She was using my name too much. Speaking too softly. Like she thought I was a fucking flight risk, and bound to run the moment she spoke above a gentle whisper. Fuck that. "If it's okay with you, I'd like to do a quick physical to ascertain what might be causing your symptoms. If you can hold still for me, it'll be over quickly and I can let you go."

Finally, we were getting somewhere.

I nodded nervously, tempted to tell her to have at it.

But I didn't.

My words were all dried up for the time being.

I let her touch me, even though the brush of her cool gloved fingers made my skin crawl all over. Scenting her discreetly, I became alarmed when I realized how easy it was to pick out the fact she was an alpha. But…she wasn't mine. So her scent was all wrong.

I wished desperately then for my scent-blindness to come back. The idea of living in a world where I was forced to smell everyone but the person I wanted was enough to make me sick to my stomach.

Just like I'd suspected, Dr. Reynolds didn't find anything wrong with me.

Not until she stumbled upon the bandage covering my bond mark, at least. With a sickening lurch, I let her peel back the bandage, terrified she'd find the bite. Even *more* terrified she'd find nothing.

"I'm assuming this bite was less than consensual," she said gently, taking a polite step back as my chest heaved and bile rose up my throat.

"*Why would you assume that?*" I hissed, offended. I knew I was being a dick, my teeth bared, my shoulders drawn high and tight, but I couldn't help it. This was my fucking alpha she was shitting all over. Sure, he wasn't perfect. But I'd wanted everything he'd ever given me, and the idea that she'd think otherwise made my skin crawl.

"Newly bonded omegas usually don't look this upset about bonding," she said gently. "They don't hide it from their doctors."

"*I'm not upset about the fucking bite mark*," I managed to bite out, though I was admittedly more than a little relieved it was still there. The itching under my skin only amplified as I slapped a hand protectively over the bite, the bumpy skin soothing me as I fingered the shape of Haden's fangs. I knew she had a point, but I couldn't help my reaction to her words.

"So it *was* consensual," she replied, clearly confused. I didn't know what to say. It wasn't really her business. Now that I'd made it clear she was wrong, talking about this with someone that wasn't Haden felt like a betrayal. Our memories together were intimate. I hadn't even given Tommy this many details and he was my favorite person ever. (Second favorite, actually.)

Haden *had* left, though.

Whatever bond we'd had was dead and gone.

He hadn't wanted me.

And I had a feeling *that* might be relevant, so I managed to force the words out, feeling alone and small inside the pristine emptiness of the clinic's exam room. "He left." The words were robbed from me, ragged and broken, my eyes blurring with heat.

"Ah," Reynolds took a seat in her chair across the room, allowing me the distance I needed as she scratched away at my clipboard. "I'm sorry to hear that."

Not as sorry as I was.

"So…" I asked after a few minutes had passed and she kept scratching away with her pen. "What's wrong with me?"

Reynolds paused, flicking a reassuring smile my way. She flipped through the pages on her clipboard one last time. There were more papers there than the ones I'd filled out in the waiting room. I wondered what they said about me. What sins they said I'd committed just by being born.

"The good news is that the problem is entirely fixable." She flashed me a reassuring smile that felt anything but that. "The bad news is that you're going to have to make a big choice."

I waited, unsure what she meant.

"It's clear to me that what you're suffering from is a bad case of bond sickness."

"Bond sickness?" I'd never heard of such a thing.

"Yes," she gave me another reassuring smile. I saw the way she reached out to soothe me, then aborted the movement at the last second, respecting the distance I'd erected between us. It had been so long since I'd been touched that my skin ached for it. But it wasn't her hands I wanted.

No.

The ones I wanted were purple and covered in scars. Long-fingered. Callused. Bigger than my own and more gentle, too. My eyes burned.

"Yes. Bond sickness is common in situations like yours."

Situations like mine? What the fuck was that supposed to mean? Sure we'd met in less than ideal circumstances. I'd been cold, and he'd been... well, he'd been something. But everything between us had felt like a dream—not the nightmare my everyday life fucking was.

The memories were precious.

Bittersweet.

But priceless all the same.

"When an alpha leaves after bonding with an omega, they both go through…" Reynolds pursed her lips thoughtfully, then relaxed. "For lack of a better word—withdrawals."

Withdrawals?

Huh.

"Like an addict?"

"Exactly so." Reynolds flashed me an indulgent smile that made my skin crawl.

"So, like—is there a pill or something I can take?" I nudged her along, "You know. So it's not so bad?" My bank account was already weeping but I was desperate to make the pain stop now that I knew there was hope.

Reynolds frowned at me, her brow furrowing for a moment before her expression smoothed. "I'm afraid it's not that simple." Her smile turned sad and my insides twisted up together. If it wasn't simple that meant it was complicated. I'd never done well with complicated things. My thoughts were spaghetti again, writhing like noodle-y snakes as my breath hitched and fear buzzed just beneath the surface of my skin. "You really only have two options."

Two options were better than no options, even *I* knew that.

"Okay?" I waited.

"You can choose to dissolve your side of the bond chemically—"

"No." I interrupted immediately. That wasn't an option. Whatever Haden had done had already broken the tendrils connecting us from his end. The idea of shredding through whatever was left with a chemical, erasing the last traces of his touch, was enough to make me vomit. "*No,*" I repeated.

"Alright," Dr. Reynolds gave me a sad smile. "The second option is the obvious." She pressed her lips together. "You can wait. Let the bond go

away on its own."

It didn't escape my notice that there didn't seem to be an option where I got to keep it.

My pulse was thrumming, my body slick with anxious sweat.

She was *useless*. There'd been no point coming here after all.

Maybe this is what Haden had meant when he'd said staying together was dangerous. Maybe he'd known we'd end up like this. Maybe…his absence was a weak attempt to protect me. That thought made me want to laugh. I didn't *need* him to protect me. I needed him to make me smile, to chase away my demons with gentle hands and the throb of his dick. I needed his scent to run through my veins, his blood in my mouth. I needed every part of him, all the time, but not this.

I couldn't just let him go.

I didn't care that holding onto him was tearing me apart.

Maybe somewhere, wherever he was—*or wasn't*—he was feeling the effects of our bond, too. Maybe he felt sick to his stomach. Maybe he ached for me the way I ached for him.

"And what if it doesn't?" I asked, my words choked. "What if the bond doesn't dissolve?"

Dr. Reynolds was silent for what felt like an eternity, her eyes overwhelmed with sadness. Pity. "You will die."

Ah.

Somehow…the idea of death didn't seem quite so scary anymore.

I knew nothingness. I knew pain. I knew what it felt like to be separated from the other half of my soul. Death?…no. Death was not the worst-case scenario.

"There's nothing else you can do?" I confirmed, one last time.

"I'm sorry." Reynolds checked the chart again, pursing her lips, like she was searching for answers we both knew weren't there. "I'll let you process all this while I run a few more tests. I don't think we're going to find anything different, but I'd like to be sure before I send you away."

I nodded numbly, docile as I let her do what she needed to do.

By the time I'd been poked with needles, prodded, and inspected, she pulled back with a frown. Even when I'd gotten my physical before being approved for the omega dorm, no one had drawn my blood, so I shouldn't have been surprised when she spoke.

"I have more bad news, unfortunately." *More bad news? Oh goodie.* "Are you taking any suppressants right now?"

I knew I should lie. But she could probably see on my chart that I'd been picking up my prescription like clockwork. Her question was a courtesy. Nothing more.

"Sometimes," I shrugged, trying to recall the last time I'd taken them. It was hilarious, actually, how I'd religiously popped pills pretty much my entire life, but the moment Haden had slipped away keeping my instincts at bay had no longer become important. "I've been forgetting lately."

"Alright." Reynolds checked her chart again, glancing at my test results with a furrow in her brow. "This can't be right," she murmured under her breath, double-checking the paper as the wrinkles on her face turned from cracks to caverns.

I already knew what she was looking at. Weirdly enough I didn't give a fuck. "It is."

She glanced up at me, her eyebrows rising as her lips drew into a thin line once again. I knew what she was looking at. Knew that the pill bottles were not adding up the way they were supposed to. Knew that she could see plain as day that I didn't need them.

"You have dangerously high levels of Alphacortiphone in your system," she said softly, though we both knew I already knew that. "This could be contributing to the fogginess you mentioned experiencing earlier. Am I correct in assuming that you haven't been taking the strongly recommended breaks between cycles?"

The way she said *strongly recommended* made it obvious the breaks weren't recommended at all. More like required.

I couldn't bring myself to care, even though she looked obviously paler than she had before. It was clear she was genuinely concerned. Which was a shame, because the emotion was wasted.

Reynolds took a deep breath. "I have good news for you then. Taking a break from suppressants and blockers will surely let your levels dip back into a normal range, which will help with some of the symptoms you've been experiencing, though not all." She flashed a cheery smile, which I didn't return. "I'm going to prescribe you a bottle that is half your usual dosage. I want you weaned off of your suppressants entirely, but we'll have to settle for this for now. At your age, if you continue abusing unnecessary, potentially harmful medicines, as you have been, your symptoms will only get worse. The fatigue and lethargy you have been experiencing are only the beginning of a long list of health issues I'm sure I don't have to repeat for you to recall your previous doctor's warning."

Lesions, internal bleeding, boils, depression, heart failure, etc.

I'd had them memorized since I was sixteen.

The consequences of my actions had always felt so far away. A problem for future me to figure out.

"You can't quit something as strong as Alphacortiphone cold turkey

so I want you to make sure you are taking the correct half-dosage." She blinked, her face shuttering with a quiet huff. "You'd think your mother would've warned you about things like this—" she muttered under her breath.

My mother?

Why would my mother warn me?

"What do you mean?" My mother was dead. She'd been dead for years, long before I'd ever presented. I could hardly remember anything about her, though I did recall the way the air had tasted like rain as we'd buried her. The white daisies I'd picked from her garden that I'd placed on top of her grave. The way Dad had brushed my hair out of my face, leaned down, and whispered in my ear, "Don't you dare embarrass me now."

So I'd swallowed my tears, just like I'd swallowed everything else.

Let myself become a black hole that sucked up all the bad and was left empty.

"It's not often I have second-generation omegas that haven't been at least taught the basics of their anatomy." She shook her head. "Your mother should've gone over all of this with you before you presented."

"Why would she do that?" It didn't make sense. No one had known I was an omega until I'd gotten slick and Dad had thrown me in the basement. Dr. Reynolds was staring at me, clearly confused as well, her head cocking as she tried to get a read on me.

"Your mother really never told you about any of this?" There was pity in her voice.

"Why would she?" It didn't make sense. "She died before I presented."

Reynolds blinked, shifting uncomfortably the way people always did when you told them your parents were dead. Like they didn't know what to do. Like they didn't know what to say, or how to treat you. I just glared at her, even though the room was spinning, spinning, *spinning* again.

"My apologies," she murmured gently.

It still didn't make sense, though. Why would my mom be educating me about my "anatomy" before I'd presented?

"No. Wait." I shook my head. "What was that other thing you said? About…you know. Second-generation, or whatever?"

Dad had always told me Mom was a beta.

"You mean…" I inferred, "my mom was an omega?"

Reynolds nodded, confirming her earlier words.

"It…*says* that?" I asked, and she nodded again.

"It's listed on your medical records."

"Can I see?"

She held the chart out to me, showing me the top of the page where my mother's and father's names lay side by side, the symbol of their designations beside them. Omega. Alpha.

What the fuck?

What the actual fuck?

Why would he lie about that?

How could I not have known?

"What did you mean? When you said she should've talked to me?" I asked, because it still didn't make sense. None of this did. Even if she was an omega, like it said, and Dad had lied to my fucking face—which wasn't that surprising—she still couldn't have known how I'd present.

"Oh." Reynolds blinked. "It's customary for parents to let their children know information like this before their presentation, so they're more prepared. Bond sickness and abuse of suppressants are more common

than you'd think."

"That doesn't make sense." I glared at her. "How would they know my designation before I presented?"

Her face twisted with pity again, the expression making me sick all over. "That's one of the first things tested during pregnancy," she said gently. "It's been a standard part of procedure for nearly a hundred years."

A hundred years?!

A hundred years they'd been running tests to figure out if babies were alphas, betas, or omegas before birth. Did that mean…*did that mean that they'd known?* That all along—*all along*…my dad had *known*?

From the moment I was pretty much conceived?

So why…

I thought back on my childhood. The way he'd treated me. The way my whole world had flipped on its head the moment I'd had my first heat. But no…*no*. As I searched through my memory, I realized *that* was all wrong.

He hadn't started mistreating me after presenting.

It had been before that, long before.

From the moment my mother had died, actually.

My stomach churned as I recalled her face, tearing through the painful fog of time as I forced myself to remember the broken blood vessels she sported—the way she carried herself like a wounded animal, the exact same way I did. Her eyes ringed black. Lips split. The way she tucked me into bed with tears clumping her lashes and bruises smudged around her wrists.

No.

He hadn't hurt me because I was an omega.

He'd hurt me because he couldn't hurt her.

SIXTEEN

PERCY

I was reeling the entire ride back to the greenhouse. Redhead, whatever her name was, looked concerned. She tried to get me to talk, but I couldn't find the words to speak. My thoughts were all jumbled up, just tangles upon tangles, as she pulled to a stop in the employee parking lot and I immediately burst out of the vehicle.

Half an hour later—sickness be damned—I was on my way to my hometown for the first time in almost a year.

Everything was shaky, my world turned upside down. But anger fueled me as I glared down the shaggy fields on either side of the road, intimidating scarecrows and farm houses, the sputter of my heart louder than the engines.

All this time.

All this time, I'd thought this was my fault.

That by shocking my dad by presenting omega, I'd committed the ultimate sin. Unforgivable in his eyes. I'd slapped Band-Aid after Band-

171

Aid on our interactions, let my love for him blind me from the truth.

The truth was, I hadn't done anything to deserve the way he treated me. There was nothing I could've done to stop it.

I'd always told myself I knew that.

But it wasn't until I realized the powerlessness of the situation that it really hit me that it was true. I'd been born an omega. Why he'd hidden that information from me, I'd never understand. Why had it taken me twenty-one fucking years to realize that he was a sad fucking man, lying to get me to excuse his behavior because he wanted to me to believe it was my fault? He'd fucking known from the second the doctors had shown him the paperwork what I was.

His excuses were just that, excuses. To cover up the fact that he was an abusive prick who thought violence was the only way to release the hate that festered like mold around his heart.

He'd made me a target, and I'd let him.

Usually, when I was angry at him, I thought of the way he laughed, the way he sat silently in his recliner, beer in hand, a smile on his lips as he watched my brothers and I beat each other's asses driving fictional cars into each other. But this time the memories didn't soothe me. His humor seemed dark now. His smile fake.

Beneath it all was a monster I had never let myself confront.

The truth was, I had no power to change him. He was, and had always been, the kind of person who used his fists to make a point. No matter what I did, no matter how I'd presented, there would've been nothing I could do to change that. I'd always been destined to be his punching bag. I could get good grades, a good job. I could hide who I was my entire fucking life, wither and fade away, hug the wall to avoid his notice—but

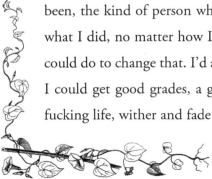

it was pointless.

Maybe I should've realized this before.

Maybe I really was as stupid as he said I was.

But I acknowledged during that whirlwind of a drive that all along I'd been hoping and praying that there was a plausible explanation behind his madness. That there was a purpose to his anger. Because I loved him, I wanted to believe that he wasn't a bad man. That it wasn't his fault I was just…*bad*.

But I knew that wasn't true now.

My car crunched along the gravel as I pulled into the driveway, ignoring the curious looks I received from the trailer next to ours. I'd spent most of high school living here. We'd lost the house just like Dad had lost his jobs, so this had become my home as much as it was my prison. After Mom died, I shared a bed with Marv and spent afternoons inhaling dry cereal and staying out of my dad's way.

A shadow in my own home.

Surviving on scraps of love because it was all I'd ever had.

Hard to know you're eating shit if you've never eaten anything else.

I stared at the missing shingles skipping like a checkerboard across the battered trailer roof. Dad's truck was missing. And my mother's flowers I'd religiously replanted along the bottom of the foundation when I was seventeen had long since withered, just brittle husks ringing the white siding like a graveyard of everything good I'd ever done here.

I sat in my car for a while, unable to bring myself to move.

Because I knew the second I did, nothing was going to be the same.

I'd never come back here.

That chapter in my life would close.

I was ready, but I was scared, too. Who was I without my father's shadow looming over me? I'd never had potential before, and it should've felt freeing, but instead the world that opened up before me was so vast it felt claustrophobic. With a ragged breath, I forced myself out of the car.

I pushed through the front door, well aware of how agitated I probably looked. Just like I'd always been a shit liar, I was spectacularly bad at hiding my emotions. As I pushed through the front door the scent inside the building hit me like a hammer. Dirt, musk, mold, plastic. I inhaled again. Marv's scent. Buck's. A handful of omegas. It felt weird to be here without the scent-blindness, and I had no doubt that the longer I stayed off the suppressants, the stronger my nose would become.

Fuck. Maybe everyone else had been right all along. Alphas *did* stink.

Not Haden, my mind supplied treacherously.

The lost feeling that had plagued me as I sat in the driveway morphed as I caught the lingering scent of blood in the air. It was old. Stale. Coppery and brittle as paper. Even without my full senses, it was clear whose blood it was.

Mine.

From the last time I'd visited.

There was bleach too, like someone had tried to cover it up, but done a shit job cleaning.

And that was when the anger hit. Like a switch flipped inside my head. Off went my fear and on went fury. *Bang.* Like fire igniting my body with its heat, I shoved past the beat-up sectional where both my brothers sat and forced my way toward the back of the house. The walls were yellowed with cigarette smoke, and more anger bubbled up as I remembered just how relieved I'd been when Dad had stopped smoking.

174

"Hey!" Marv called from his spot on the couch. He paused his video game, more than a little confused as he and Buck both twisted around to greet me. It wasn't their fault. None of this was. But I couldn't help but let my anger bleed toward them as I shoved into my old shared bedroom and began throwing my childhood shit into an empty laundry basket I emptied of Marv's dirty clothes.

I heard footsteps behind me, but I ignored them, emptying the closet of my few remaining belongings, pulling open drawers, my breathing heavy, my movements jerky.

"What are you doing?" Marv asked from the doorway. I could hear the TV again. Buck was out there, probably flipped it back on the moment he realized nothing was amiss. He'd always been a bit blind to emotions, which I'd found endearing usually, but at the moment I just felt...sad.

He probably wouldn't get why I was leaving.

Leaving Dad meant leaving them too.

Maybe they weren't the best brothers. Maybe they'd bullied me a bit too much when we were kids. But they were still mine, and I was still leaving them behind.

Marv's brown eyes were big and sad, his massive body blocking the door frame as I swiped my old cleats into the laundry basket and turned back around. He was bigger than me, but only in height. We'd all gotten Dad's build, though Dad's body had withered with age and his gut had grown from the amount of beer he chugged. Marv and Buck both had Mom's eyes, and the jealousy that thought aroused inside me made my palms slick with anger.

I didn't say anything, just stepped forward, my nostrils flaring as I tried to shove past him.

"I'm talking to you, Percy." Marv shifted to block the door, forcing me to duck the other way. Back and forth we went. We'd done this dance before, but it had never made me this irrationally pissed off. I glared at the ketchup stain on his shirt, the scent of corn dogs clinging to his skin. He hadn't shaved. Or showered. He reeked.

My nose wrinkled.

When it was clear I wasn't going to talk, he let me pass, clearly confused by my anger as I stormed my way into the kitchen. There were a few of Mom's things here. Maybe it was selfish of me to collect the last of her tea set, or the two porcelain bowls she'd paid ten bucks for at the thrift store so she could dress up our pitiful fucking Christmas dinners, but I did it anyway. It'd started as a full set, and Dad's tantrums had shattered piece by piece till this was all that was left.

Two fucking dishes.

Coated in dust and full of the husks of dead bugs that had burrowed inside where they lay forgotten at the back of the cupboard.

"Dad's almost home if you want to see him," Buck called from the couch, clearly oblivious. Marv was still watching me, he'd always been the smarter of the two. I could smell his confusion, and the overwhelming scent made my head spin. I wasn't used to this. *Any of it*. It was so strong—so…fuck. The anger, too, felt unfamiliar.

Maybe I'd gotten something more than black eyes from my dad after all.

I needed to get out of here before Dad came home.

I didn't know what he'd do to me if he found out what I was planning, and I wasn't about to find out.

Dad's almost home if you want to see him, Buck's words echoed in my

head. A warning.

"I don't," I grunted. *That* unsurprisingly got Buck's attention. Everyone knew I was a complete fucking suck-up. It had been the only way to survive. And maybe in a way, I'd hoped it would make a difference. That my devotion would mean something to him.

But it was just as meaningless as his love was.

"What's got your panties in a twist?" Buck had risen at some point, joining Marv in the doorway to the kitchen. They looked like twins, probably because they were. Their dark hair stuck out at odd angles, their brown eyes flooded with mystified concern as I pushed through their bodies and into the living room toward the front door.

Diving in front of me, Buck blocked my way, Marv joining him a moment later.

"Move," I growled, my earlier anger still buzzing like poison in my veins.

"Dude, what the fuck?" Buck raised his hands placatingly. He still had grease smudged across them from his last shift at the auto shop, but even that familiar sight wasn't comforting. If I glanced to the right, I knew I'd see his Playstation controller sitting on the couch where he'd left it, just as stained as his hands. Familiar. Reminding me of all the good times I hadn't known were shit until now.

The longer I stayed here, the scarier it became to dive into the unknown. Little reminders of what I was leaving behind bittersweet.

"What's going on?" Marv tried, piping in more gently. He'd always been softer than Dad and Buck. He'd bullied me as much as Buck had, but he'd at least been a bit apologetic about it. He lived by his own set of morals, even if they were slightly twisted.

"Percy's being a grade-A douche-nozzle." Buck rolled his eyes, glaring

at me. "That's what's going on."

"I am *not*," I hissed, desperate to get out of there before shit really hit the fan.

Any second now, Dad could walk through the back door, and I'd be fucked.

"Then what's your deal?" they both asked at the same time.

"You're in my way, and I'm trying to leave." I tried to shove through them, only for Buck to shove me back, a mean twist to his lips I hadn't seen in years. He'd never treated me more gently because I was an omega, despite living by an outdated sense of chivalry. In that moment, I was glad for the equality, glad I didn't have to feel bad about hitting him if this fight took itself to a physical level.

If I had to punch my way through both of them, I would.

"Fuck off," I glared at him and he raised his hands again, flashing a second confused look at Marv. This wasn't like me. They both knew it. I was the peacemaker, the quiet one. The one who took the hits silently, letting the world blur, and his tears die before they were ever born to begin with.

Marv made a face of realization and nodded toward me, "He's trying to get out of here before Dad shows up."

Idiots.

"Oh." Buck's concern turned wicked. "You're probably right. Fuck." He grinned at Marv, gleeful. "What do you think he did?"

I could feel the way my body shook, my anger boiling over. The grip I had on the laundry basket slipped a little, and unable to think of an alternative, I braced myself to lose the last things that meant anything to me. With Haden's jacket too tight across my shoulders, I dropped

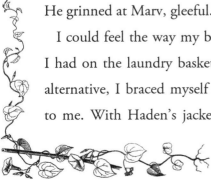

the basket, watching almost in slow motion as both my brothers' eyes widened and they dropped like potatoes down to catch it before it hit the floor, effectively clearing the way to the door.

"What the fuck, Percy?!" Buck huffed, basket clutched in his arms. I wound around them both, only inches from the doorknob before Marv dove in front of it again, fury twitching the muscle at the corner of his jaw. I almost wished he'd punch me, just so I could punch back. But then the worst possible thing happened.

The back door opened with a familiar *creak*.

And just like that, all my anger melted away and a lifetime of fear came back full force.

SEVENTEEN

PERCY

I could smell Dad before I saw him. Taste the bitter heat of his anger in the air as it traveled on the breeze that wafted in behind him before the back door shut with a loud click. Suddenly, I was grateful for all those years I'd spent without being able to fully taste his hate in the air, or the scent of my own resulting fear.

The stench was overwhelming.

"What the hell is going on?" Dad was a man of few words. He always had been. So when he asked a question, we'd all learned we better answer. Promptly too.

Two seconds.

It only took two seconds for my world to fall apart.

On instinct, I backed into Marv, the movement jostling us both as my gaze flickered to his face and I watched in slow motion as everything fell apart. His breath hitched and his eyes widened. The scent of our fear mingled, and that thought made me sick. *Why was he looking at me like*

that? My confusion evolved when I realized what exactly it was he was staring at.

It wasn't Dad.

It wasn't Buck.

It was me.

My neck.

My goddamn fucking *naked* neck.

I slapped a hand over my bare bond bite, terrified when the touch of my bare palm confirmed my worst fears had come true. After a year of meticulous caution I'd finally, inevitably fucked myself over. I'd never replaced the bandage the doctor had removed earlier.

I'd been too angry to think as I'd stormed my way over here to end things for good.

And now my worst nightmare was about to become reality.

"Percy," Marv said, his voice small and sad. And that simple utterance of my name made a cold chill run through my body. He'd never said my name like that before. Forlorn. Like he was mourning me already. I'd fucked up. He knew it. I knew it. We both knew the outcome of this, and I could already picture both my brothers in black, my grave devoid of flowers because neither of them had ever had Mom's green thumb.

The second Dad saw the bite, I was as good as dead.

And it was inevitable now.

There was silence.

My pulse was a steady staccato.

Thump, thump, thump.

Lap, lap, lap went the water that licked at my toes.

It only took another second for me to realize that covering the bite with my hand had been the stupidest thing I'd ever done. Maybe I could've gotten away with it. With ignoring it. Dad was almost ten feet away. If he hadn't gotten any closer, he may never have even noticed. But, like an idiot, I'd brought attention to the mark—and all it took was one rough inhale from behind me for me to realize I was a dead man.

"Oh, Percy." Marv's voice was laced with sadness as I met his gaze and we both turned toward the oncoming storm. My mother's soft brown eyes looked back at me from his face. Full of pity, regret, fear. But not for him. No. *For me*. Regret for what was about to happen, and the fact he couldn't stop it. Looking at Dad now was like staring at an oncoming train. But I couldn't help myself. I tipped my head up and met his eyes. Fear unlike anything I'd ever felt before drowned my lungs till they were waterlogged and my throat and ears were clogged.

Buck stood up, clearly sensing something bad had happened. "What?" He turned to look at me, immediately zeroing in on the hand I still had clutching my bond mark protectively. Remorse flooded his gaze as well, and he turned back to face Dad, his broad shoulders stiff.

"It doesn't mean anything," I said quietly, old habits rising to the surface. Placate, apologize, survive. It didn't feel like a lie either. It didn't mean anything. It meant *everything*. There was a difference.

"It doesn't mean anything, Dad." Marv agreed quickly. His bulk still blocked the door, and I knew I only had seconds to escape if I was going to get a head start. There was no doubt my dad would give chase. I'd tarnished his property, after all. Done the one thing he told me he'd never forgive. This would end in blood, and weirdly enough the thought soothed me.

The promise of violence was familiar.

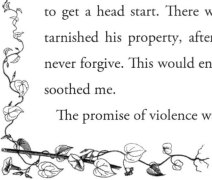

At least for me.

Falling into fear felt like coming home.

Marv still blocked my only exit.

Move, move, move, I pleaded with my eyes, but Marv was still staring at Dad, not me.

"It doesn't mean anything," he repeated. "Right, Percy?"

I didn't know what else to say. I'd already spoken my piece. I could lie over and over but we all knew this would only end one way. Marv's lips thinned as he waited, and the longer I sat in silence, the more the sadness in his eyes morphed into something else. Resignation.

The doorknob clicking open was far too loud in the awkward silence, but it wasn't my hand that had turned it.

Marv's big brown eyes said goodbye as he shoved the door open, and Buck turned around in one swift twist to shove me out of it.

The last glimpse I had of either of them as I stumbled down the steps was one I'd seen often enough as a kid. Broad shoulders side by side. A mirrored silhouette as they squared off against my dad, and the door that I'd kept open on this chapter of my life slid shut with finality.

I couldn't go home. Not when Dad knew where I lived. Tommy was out of the question. I refused to be the reason he got hurt—because I knew he wouldn't hesitate to jump in front of my dad to save me. So I didn't visit him either.

Logic dictated I run a different course.

But the real reason I chose my destination was because despite the fact

that logic should dictate my decision, my heart had decided instead.

I could see Dad's pickup truck in my rear view mirror. No matter how many turns I made, how many lights I blasted through, he was always there. Like a phantom haunting me. The way he had my entire fucking life.

Chipped blue paint.

Hazel eyes, just like my own, that brought me to Hell when I looked inside them.

As I parked my car in the gravel, I paused for a second to reflect on my own stupidity. I knew what I was doing was genuinely idiotic, running to an isolated location just because the omega inside me was chasing comfort from a man that had disappeared from my life. Haden's jacket was bunched too tight around my shoulders as my feet hit the pebbles with a crunch and I left the car running behind me so I wouldn't waste precious seconds as I tore off across the graveyard.

It was just as barren here as it had been the last time I'd visited.

The sun had sunk low on the horizon, disappearing behind the mountains. My headlights bleeding across tombstones, illuminating the way as I dodged long-dead bodies, and prayed to whatever Gods were listening that I could get away. That I could find *him*.

That he'd give me back the choice he'd taken away to save me.

It was cold.

The kind of cold that takes bites from your flesh and burrows deep inside the marrow of your bones. Icy. Mean. Painful in its winter flavored vitriol.

They said the Devil came out on winter nights just like this one. That the passage to Hell was only a few short steps away. Hidden behind tombstones and half-wilted bouquets at the back of a graveyard older

184

than the town itself.

They said the Devil visited those that were most vulnerable.

They said the Devil took what he wanted to take.

If I was a smarter guy, I would've run away. Run far from Haden's offer uttered under the blanket of darkness. Run away from the promise of a forever too long to comprehend. But...I was stupid.

And I wanted the Devil to take me.

The bridge was right ahead. Twenty more yards and I'd be there. The trees loomed larger with every step. I didn't know what would happen when I arrived beneath it, only able to guess, as my blood thrummed with fear—and purpose—and the crackle of leaves behind me alerted me to the fact that my dad was right on my heels.

I could smell him.

His anger, bitter and sharp. Like dried blood and burnt aluminum.

Dad wasn't faster than me on a normal day.

But even with adrenaline rushing through my body, there was nothing I could do about the weakness that had eaten away my bones and chipped away at my energy for the past few months. I couldn't get away. I stumbled, the sluggishness coming back with a vengeance right at the worst possible moment. I was too slow.

Too fucking slow.

Too slow to realize I was in danger.

Too slow to realize the lie I was trapped inside.

Too slow to keep the man I'd decided was mine.

Ten yards left.

Halfway there.

Ten yards.

Ten yards that felt like ten miles as I stumbled over abandoned tombstones and tripped over my own feet. My toes caught on something as I approached the jagged rocks that lined the edge of the graveyard. The ground rushed up toward my face. Heat burned at the back of my neck as I scrambled toward the rocks. So close. So fucking close. If I could only grab a weapon—

Dirt clung to my knees and shins, and my toes and fingers were numb.

The scent of dead things permeated the air. Rotting leaves and decay, like an exhale between winter's first harsh, life-sucking kisses.

The sun had sunk below the horizon ages ago.

But stubbornly, I'd still come.

A man arriving at the gallows, ready to be delivered to the Devil he craved.

A hand met the back of my neck.

Nails bit into my flesh, the hot huff of breath on the shell of my ear my only warning as I was shoved face first into the dirt and a massive body climbed on top of mine. I couldn't breathe. Crushed beneath his weight, Dad was strong despite his age, and I struggled, scrambling for something—anything I could latch onto.

The moon steadily rose, its silvery caress painting the smattering of rocks in front of me. Some big, some small. Moss covered. Dirty. I'd gotten close enough. Oh god.

Pain, pain, *pain*.

I cried out, a broken sound that echoed through the quiet. Crickets stopped chirping. The wind no longer whistled. There was a rock in my hand. It scraped its gritty edges against my skin as I was flipped over and finally caught the glint of hatred that boiled blood-red behind my dad's eyes.

I stared but I didn't recognize him.

His skin was sallow, his lips drawn thin. There was a sickness in his eyes that stole away the last bits of the man I had forced myself to love.

When you get married, you get to choose to love someone for life. They do this whole stupid thing where you recite vows you didn't write for yourself, and you nod along, making promises you know you don't have to keep.

My love for my dad had never been like that.

It wasn't a paper I could sign.

It wasn't something I could divorce myself from.

But this...*this* person above me—as he wrapped his hands around my neck and my mind stuttered as it sputtered for oxygen—*this* was not my father.

And at that moment, I realized I hated him.

I hated him so *fucking* much.

Hated him for what he'd done to me.

Hated him for what he'd done to my mom.

For the endless cycle of pain that wouldn't end even if he killed me.

Hated him for the life he'd stolen from me, the life he was intent on stealing.

But most of all, I hated him, because he had forced me into a corner. Forced me to make a decision I never thought I'd have to make.

I hated him because he had given me no choice.

So I smashed the rock into his temple.

Three hits.

The sick crunch of bone.

The sharp scent of copper.

My pills rattled in my pocket as I brought my fist down, over and over.

Three hits was all it took to slay my demon.

Finally, it was over. His body slumped, and I gasped for air the moment his grip on my neck grew slack. The throbbing in my head eased momentarily as I clawed at his limp body, trying to get him off of me. He was heavy. And I was weak. The scent of stale beer and sickness wafted from his flesh as I shoved, and shoved, and *shoved*.

No matter how hard I tried, I couldn't find the strength to move him.

My head was on fire, my body numb.

That itching sensation beneath my skin returned, churning my stomach and leeching all my strength as I lay beneath his bulk and finally gave up.

With my chest compressed and blood dripping onto the hollow of my throat from his head wound, I stared up at the moon. I watched it rise steadily, unaffected by the brutality of what I'd just done. The darkness closed around me, choking the last bit of my energy away as I let the anger I'd buried for years simmer inside my hardened heart.

I'd thought with him gone I'd feel better.

But I didn't.

I couldn't breathe, and I wasn't sure if it was because he was still crushing me—even in death—or if it was because the relief I'd thought I'd feel with him dead was still just out of reach. I shouldn't mourn him, but I did. I couldn't help it.

I lost time.

Seconds.

Minutes.

Hours.

The moon was high in the sky for a moment, low the next, the last vestiges of silver slipping away as the sun began its ascent. Dad was heavy on top of me. Cold now. The scent of his body decomposing, enough to make me gag. I didn't know what would happen now. I hadn't thought I'd win, even though this didn't really feel like winning.

Part of me had even hoped I would die, putting an end to my suffering, but I hadn't.

Like a cockroach, I'd somehow survived.

I lost more time.

Not much.

But enough.

Because when I opened my eyes again, the sun was barely creeping over the tree line. It was warmer now. And I could breathe easier, though I realized belatedly that the reason my chest was no longer compressed was because my dad's corpse had been moved. I glanced around weakly, trying to figure out where the hell it could've gone, if this was just another hallucination.

But it wasn't.

Familiar fingers carded through my hair.

Like a rubber band, I snapped. My head twisted back, my throat clogged up, my eyes burning as I caught the blurry shape of a familiar mask. The silhouette of my favorite broad shoulders.

"I forgot the living could be so cruel," Haden's voice was a balm over the itchy heat that tore through my body like wildfire. I laughed, the sound jostling my sore chest, before it morphed into a sob.

Sunlight made his mostly white hair glow, turning him into an avenging angel.

"Have you made your choice?" He kept stroking my hair, gently, reverently. Like he didn't know what to do with me. Didn't know what to do with the mess I'd become.

I didn't blame him. I didn't know what to do either.

All I knew was that I was so *angry* at him. So fucking angry. He'd left me, after all. But I couldn't bring myself to speak, or do much of anything, really. I chased his eyes behind the shadows of his mask, tracing over the familiar contours of the skull. For a moment, I caught his gaze, and I was trapped inside it. Concern. Syrupy-sweet. Anger simmering just under the surface.

I'd never seen him angry before, and judging by the gentle brush of his fingers in my hair, I never would've guessed it was there at all. But it was. Like a fire that waged war beneath the surface of his actions.

"If you do not answer, then I will make the choice for you," Haden warned.

I didn't want to choose.

I didn't want to do anything.

I just didn't want him to stop petting me. As angry as I was, I was relieved, too. At my lowest, he was here, just as I'd hoped he would be. I didn't know what the future held for us. I was too tired to care. But I was glad he was here, even if he was a purple-demon-fuck-boy who'd ghosted me.

"Fine." Haden's tone was final, his rumbling voice echoing through the rapidly closing space between us as he bent down, and in one swift move had me pulled up into his arms. I took a moment to be impressed, considering the fact we were nearly the same size. Him, tall and lean; me, shorter and thicker.

His steps didn't stumble, his breath didn't stutter.

So I let the smug asshole carry me, too weak to hold myself up, as I watched the shadows beneath the bridge creep toward us. His chest heaved, and I pressed my nose against the hollow of his throat, inhaling his scent clearly for the first time.

It was earthy.

Like a damp cave.

Like soil in the spring or wet pavement. Inhaling greedily, I relaxed when his arms tightened incrementally around me in response, his chest rumbling his approval. As the shadows slid closer, it occurred to me that this was it. I knew I could ask him to take me back, that it might be my last chance to do so. My last chance to chase the sunlight rising slowly behind me.

But...I didn't.

Instead, I looked forward, falling into the slippery grasp of the shadows as Haden's nose brushed my sweaty temple, and the ache that had made a home inside my chest began to slowly ease. I'd thought I didn't have much to give, but as we disappeared inside the darkness one last, final time, I realized I'd been wrong.

I just wished if I was going to Hell, I'd had the forethought to bring a six pack of Mountain Dew.

UNTIL NEXT TIME . . .

THE DEVIL TAKES

WILL RETURN IN BOOK 2

WHAT'S WILLINGLY GIVEN

Where we'll get to see more of Haden and Percy
as well as explore the realm of Hell and all its occupants.

AUTHOR'S NOTE

HELLO EVERYONE! THANK YOU SO MUCH for picking up *The Devil Takes*. This book was so much fun to create despite giving me a run for my money at the beginning. I am so happy with how it turned out and I hope you will enjoy it.

This book has darker elements in it as well as frequent references to terminology commonly used in omegaverse novels. I've included a glossary at the beginning for anyone who is unfamiliar with omegaverse and is looking to dive in for the first time. There is also a full content list on my website so you know what you're getting into before you dive in. I can't wait to hear what you all think! As always, feel free to reach out to me while you're reading, and all reviews, comments, and shares are greatly appreciated.

If you'd like to keep in touch with me and receive free content including a free ebook of *There's a Monster in the Woods* and exclusive chapters of my serial *Cloudy with a Chance of Dildos*, you can sign up at faelovesart. com/newsletter. Or join my Facebook group, Fae's Faves! You can also find me on Instagram @fae.loves.art and on Patreon.

I love you all so much, enjoy!

Special Thanks

SPECIAL THANKS to all of those that made the creation of this book possible. Especially Molly, who listened to my creative rants, and Dori who painstakingly poured over every word the second I wrote them. Thank you to everyone who contributed time, energy, and love into this, I am so grateful to call you all my friends. And thank you, to the reader, because without you the creation of this project would have been meaningless. I love you all so much.

-FAE

About Fae

FAE IS OBSESSED with anything romance. From a young age she realized she had a passion for falling in love over and over again. She loves to tell stories through both her art and writing. With a passion for classical monsters, meet-cutes, and contemporary romance you can often find her with her nose stuck in a book and her pet corgi Champa on her lap.

She currently resides in Utah with her amazing husband and her collection of squishmallows. When you read one of her books you can expect to find love stories between humans, monsters, and loveable assholes that will make you laugh (and cry) as you get lost in their worlds for just a little. Every story comes with a happy ever after guarantee.

Find her online at:

WWW.FAELOVESART.COM

Ingram Content Group UK Ltd.
Milton Keynes UK
UKHW041434160523
421839UK00004B/217